Relentless
Reminiscence

Vincent Young

I still find each day too short for all the thoughts
I want to think, all the walks I want to take,
all the books I want to read, and all the friends
I want to see.

\- John Burroughs

Struggling to think back to
The times from my past,
To remember all the love
I experience from people
Now dead and gone,
To recall the pains that
I endured through the
Adversity of my life.
Watching the candle burn,
Slowly dying in the face of fire,
All I remember is that
The loss of person after person,
Chipped away at my innocence,
And now I feel bare and exposed,
As I struggle to think back,
And recover these memories.
I barely notice my surroundings,
And I'm not afraid to be seen,
Refuse to give up on my past,
And people look upon me
In my openly displayed
Relentless reminiscence.

Relentless Reminiscence

Vincent Young

Sea of Illusion
Press

Published by Sea of Illusion Press
Copyright © 2011 by Vincent Young

This novel is a work of fiction. Any names, characters, places, and incidents either are the product of the author's imagination or are used fictitiously, and their resemblance, if any, to real-life counterparts is entirely coincidental.

ISBN-13: 978-1456570033

Printed and bound in the USA

8 7 6 5 4 3

This novel is dedicated to all
of those who inspire me and
who smiled for me when I couldn't:
my friends, readers, and supporters alike.

Prologue

Slamming the door to his room, he tumbled down onto his bed, and the tears had already begun to fall. Streaked down his face, his eyes swollen, he closed them and lay down, as sleep put him under in less than a minute. Slight retribution for what he had been put through earlier that day.

Damian - his short jet-black hair a mess upon his head, his endlessly deep brown eyes closed, peacefully so. The long lank figure of a teenage boy in his senior year, bundled up on his bed, unmoving now, his chest calmly rising and falling. Deep breaths.

Dreamless sleep would be his best friend for the next few days: this would be his only escape from the pain that would follow the memories of the last few years. Such a long time, June 20th, 4 summers ago, he had first seen her. What that had felt like though, was lost, with the time.

In the middle of the night, after lying down in the dark, wondering for one merciless minute where things had gone wrong, he mentally plotted them out, the possibilities.

Why it had happened, he still didn't know. He had been happy, but didn't the same apply to her? The present, the nights out... weren't they what she had wanted? She had smiled. Maybe not at him, but she had smiled so widely, her perfect, white teeth.

For the last week, it had all seemed just fine. Casually exchanged *I love you*'s, warm embraces while watching a movie. He would remember these all, the past few days.

Five days ago, she'd dropped by, waving politely at his father on the way in.

Four days, they had walked through the park, smiling at their reflections in the pond.

Three days, hands held, watching a movie in the theatre, sharing popcorn.

Two days, dinner with her mother, busily chattering about what activity they might partake in later. Him included, a part of them.

Just one day ago, at the mall outside of town, window shopping, sharing a coffee.

But what was the problem? Every day, she refused to look into his eyes. She shut them tightly as they kissed, looked away as they walked, linking hands. Inevitably the day had been coming though, and he had probably realized. Deep down inside, realized, that she was going to break his heart.

Chapter 1

"Rise and shine!"

Suddenly a ray of sunshine fell across the tiny crack of his eyes that he was willing to show at 6 in the morning.

"Come on, get ready, we're going out for a sprint."

Rolling over to face the door, Damian just managed to catch a glimpse of his overly energetic Asian father jogging out of his bedroom. *Having old men suddenly concerned about their weight sure can get annoying.* Especially when *your* physical wellbeing and "enjoying" your youthful years suddenly seems to be so much more important to your dad. *How does he expect me to be happy though?* That was out of the question... only 3 months ago – but there was no need to think like that.

"Guess I'm going to have to get used to this," Damian mumbled, as he sat up on his bed and looked over his entire room.

This room had been his since seven years ago, tiny and crammed, filled with sentimental bits and pieces from his past. The closet, jam-packed with clothes that no longer fit, also hiding his guitar. The bookshelf – novels strewn all over the smooth wood surface of each of the shelves. A torn picture blown by the wind under his bed... and he was comforted by the thought that he would be able to leave it behind soon. But clearly not soon enough.

Walking towards the bathroom door, taking extra care to grumble loudly as he slammed it shut, he started to brush his teeth - teeth that had been straight for the longest time, a nice complement to his flawless sand-coloured skin.

And he hated it all, how so many people would stare at him all the time, absentmindedly looking him up and down. He just couldn't stand it anymore.

Everyone noticed him, wanted to be around him... but there was one person who didn't look at him. Refused to look at him. And so, he closed his eyes, spit out the toothpaste, and rinsed.

"Isn't the breeze just so refreshing? No bugs at this time of day, perfect."

That was all his father had to say to him to let him know to tune out. Damian knew that the rest of his morning would be spent ignoring everything his father said to him, and just running. Running down the roads, feeling the wind blow against his legs, feeling the heat of the sun on the back of his neck. His dad *did* have a point in saying that this was refreshing though.

While rounding the last block, Damian sped up, in a hurry to get back home to change out of his sweaty clothes and grab his books from the various dark corners in his room.

His chemistry textbook, his copy of King Lear, his binder – but he would leave his notebook behind yet again. This notebook had held all his feelings that he could not share with anyone else for the past 4 years.

At first, it was something of a diary: him writing down all his ideas, how he was going to ask Cindy out, and how it had happened the next month, then the next. The contents of his notebook changed after the first six months though – he had run out of things to say, run out of feelings to blatantly express, sentences that he wanted to speak. This was when the poetry began.

10

Verse after verse, with a little prose in between, his beautiful pen strokes lining the pages, top to bottom, left to right. Though he had stopped for roughly 2 years in between, about a year ago, each and every day, he would spend the time to write in his notebook. This notebook contained his heart, and in his heart, he closely held his notebook.

A few months previously though, when he had his heart broken, he set down his notebook in the corner of his room by his bedside table, hidden away, now gathering dust. His flowing language, the artful use of words he had admired so much – it stopped.

Checking the time quickly, he decided that he had enough time to sit down for a minute and absorb himself in whichever day he opened the notebook up to, and remember where the words had come from, what his mind had done to make himself satisfied. To relive his emotions.

He was afraid of going back too far though, so, playing it safe, he decided to go somewhere in the middle, a good distance away from his emotionless fantasies in the final year, and from the love drunk beginning to this long, long journey that lead to how he was today.

Running his finger along the neatly formed letters as he immersed himself in the past, he began.

Water drifts down the river,
Free to travel where it may,
And I wonder where it wants to go,
Where it will end up, I cannot say.

In this water I see a reflection,
In likeness of my heart,
The desires of which, I do not know,
Its dangerous course I cannot chart.

Producing the solution,
To this trivial situation,
To know the ending to this river of my heart,
I must prevent deviation.

Now I see what must be done,
And know what there is to do,
I seal away my flowing heart,
And now to this glass, it shall stay true.

The poem, lacking a title, or a date, fascinated him. When did he write this, and where had his inspiration come from? Smiling faintly, he remembered the day 2 years ago during the summer, while Cindy was in Florida, when he had seen a cute girl pass before him. At this time, he was still a hopeless romantic, and that was something he could not change.

Obviously, he could feel his heart sway, and suddenly felt the urge to write poetry. It made him wonder though: what was really happening in his life at that time... and where did this poem come from, in the midst of all his other euphoric love poems? Taking one quick glance at the clock again, it was 7:20am, and time to go.

Setting down the notebook where he had found it and slinging his bag over his back, he ran out of his room, in a rush to get to school and find his friends where they would undoubtedly be: standing outside his homeroom class. And also without a doubt, they would all be finishing the chemistry homework due today. One final glance at his notebook, and he left the room.

The notebook's cover, he would recall when he got to school, had been of Cindy's design. The person who had made him so happy for years – and all the pain went away for a second, as he thought back... back so long ago. He thought back to four years ago, when they had taken the picture that was now the cover of his notebook: their hands, linked, in front of the open waters of Perten's local lake, Hunter Lake, the sunlight shining down, and words inscribed at the bottom of the picture: "Live the life you've dreamed – Cindy Lau and Damian Huong, forever."

Chapter 2

Students clogging up the hallways, the constant ringing of the dismissal bell droning out the surrounding conversations, chatter radiating throughout the school - the day was over.

Damian pushed through the masses steadily, making his way towards the door, desperate to hurry home, to lie down, to relax. When he finally got out the door, about to casually walk around the block and then make a full-out sprint back to his house, someone tapped him on the back.

"Hey Damian! Wanna come over to my place? We could go hang for a while, maybe catch a movie if you want," said Nicholas Chan, someone who Damian honestly preferred not to be seen with, and gave him all the more reason to hurry up and get home.

"Nah, it's alright. Maybe some other time, okay? I have to get some studying in for exams" said Damian, excusing himself from the conversation, the only thought on his mind to get home as soon as possible.

"Oh… okay then, yeah, maybe some other time… Good luck."

"Thanks. Bye."

Glad that's over. Damian jogged at a steady pace down Main St. and onto the street of his house. Maple Valley Road. Obviously implicit of somewhere beautiful, his street lived up to its name: the maple trees standing tall over any passersby, the leaves offering shade to any and all on the sidewalks, the grass a healthy shade of green as if there were pastures between the houses' driveways. Any sheep's dream.

Rounding the last bend, he stepped in front of his house, number 88, a number lucky enough to be a cause for buying a lottery ticket when they had moved in 10 years ago. Fitting his key in the door, turning it slowly, he immediately saw the note on the kitchen table, obviously addressed to him, with an excuse as to why his dad wasn't home.

Meticulously untying the standard double knot he regularly tied his shoes with in the morning, careful not to change the length of the strings, he felt his blood slowly rushing to his head. Sometimes he wondered if he had OCD, just because he took so much care with things that other people would find irrelevant. So many things he wondered about.

Slipping off his shoes and placing them on the shelf, he took long strides over to where the note lay on the kitchen countertop. A quick glance at the note told him that his father had been in a hurry to get out of the house, his letters long, loopy.

The note was just a tiny consideration of Damian, to let him know that dinner would only have to be made for himself.

Though he was starving, Damian decided to run upstairs, take a long, warm shower, and then, perhaps find yet another poem to revive some old memories.

A quick scan of the room told him that finding clean clothes might be a challenge, so he quickly threw everything in his laundry basket, and went through his closet.

Nothing he would wear outside, but, seeing as he would only be in his house, he found himself an old t-shirt from a camp he went to, some fresh underpants, and an old pair of track pants, one of the 3 pairs he still had left.

15

Grabbing his towel on the way out, he shut the door to the bathroom, opened the lights, and started running the water, imagining how it would feel to have the water running down his back in a few minutes, and to just completely lose himself in his thoughts.

Stepping into the shower, he just let the water rinse him over, and began to lather shampoo into his hair. Showering had always been a comforting process for him, mindlessly cleansing himself, singing if there was no one else home, mechanically drying himself off, then stepping outside, walking into his room. Today would be no different.

After sitting down and staring at the front of his notebook for about an hour, tears running down his face again, Damian put it down again. The feeling of this was too familiar… perhaps some other day.

He stood up suddenly and he limped out of his room, the blood only starting to return to his left leg from the awkward way he had sat with his legs crossed. Sat and stared, for so long.

Dinner started to seem pretty inviting, so he walked downstairs, took some leftover shrimp and broccoli from last night's dinner, tossed it in a bowl with rice, and put it in the microwave, timed for 2 minutes.

Quickly walking around, grabbing himself some cutlery, pouring himself some water, he suddenly missed his mother. Her passing, 3 years after they had moved into this house, 7 years ago, just 3 weeks before his 10th birthday: he still remembered it so clearly.

She had been hospitalized for a while at that point, and the prospects didn't look good for her, but every time Damian and his father visited her, she told them that they should live on, and that she would watch them from above, that she would wait for them, but that they shouldn't rush to go see her.

Suddenly, a loud beeping sound brought him back to reality: the microwave telling him that his dinner was ready.

He grabbed the bowl quickly, setting it down on the table as quickly as possible, not wanting to burn himself.

Quickly taking a bite, two bites, three bites, he wolfed it all down - he hadn't realized he was so hungry until he could smell the food.

In less than 10 minutes, he had devoured his entire dinner, and he shuddered at the disapproval his father would have had of him, not allowing time for digestion, starving himself and then eating excessively.

Damian brought his dishes over to the sink, dumping them there, planning to wash them later.

He ran upstairs again, into his room. He sat there, determined to read more of his old writing, to remember more of what his life had been like years ago, those memories preserved in the precious pages of his notebook.

Picking up the notebook again, and staring at the cover, he started to feel sick. And that's when he knew he couldn't take it.

Setting down the notebook, he turned and walked away towards the bathroom to brush his teeth, to get to bed. "Maybe some other day." What was wrong with him?

Chapter 3

"I'm sorry, I just… I feel like we need to take the time to get to… to know other people…" she stuttered, the words barely audible, "I hope you understand… it's not your fault, really… it's just… I just… I don't really know anymore. Bye, Damian."

In his mind, he could still see it – see her turning and walking away, her voice echoing in his mind. Exactly how it happened. He kept dreaming of it, thinking about it, reliving that moment over and over again, every time he saw her.

"Get to know other people…" This thought bugged him the most, but he didn't know why. Was it because he couldn't imagine she might have loved someone else? Was it the fact that right now, it was a possibility that she *did* love someone else?

"It's not your fault…" What was it that he had done? He had already spent every minute of his spare time with her. Was he missing something? Wasn't she happy?

"Bye, Damian…" and her voice reverberated in his mind, the tintinnabulation of every syllable pounding within his head, her lovely voice, speaking such… such nauseating words. He couldn't imagine how it was possible, but he kept thinking it over. "Bye, Damian…"

And he woke up. Sitting upright in a second, he stared at his wall. The calendar posted there, blandly suspended by a nail, the dates crossed out. The date was May 28th, and 3:00am according to his alarm clock on his bedside table.

Rubbing his eyes dully, he debated going back to sleep, or waking up then and feeling like a zombie for the rest of the day.

Wondering what he would do if he were to choose to stay up, he stared around his room in the dark, identifying the silhouettes of objects. Off to his left, facing away from his window now, the moonlight managing to seep into the crack in his curtains, he saw his bookshelf illuminated, some of his favourite titles in the shadow of the top shelf, his favourite childhood books were fully visible from his perspective.

For a second, the Cat in the Hat winked at him, and he couldn't help but smile.

Looking to the right of the bookshelf, he saw his closet door, slightly ajar, the arm of a jacket poking out – a jacket he identified as his first skiing jacket ever, one that hadn't fit him for the last 9 years, but also one he didn't want to pack away into a box and forget about. As the ski tags swayed slowly in the dark, he looked elsewhere, looking at the surface of his bedside table now.

He spotted his lamp, his alarm clock: an analog clock, of course, just like his watch sitting next to it. Quite strangely, he read time faster in analog than digital: most people found this fascinating, but this was just the way he had grown up. And he liked the look of clock hands so much more than LED numbers glowing lifelessly at him.

Watching the hands as they touched, the clock reading 3:16am now, he wondered why this interested him so much. He guessed the idea fascinated him, how the hands seemingly went round and round, taking forever to make the trip to meet each other, but the meeting only lasting a minute.

VINCENT YOUNG

Quality time, spent unmoving, together as one, until the time tears them apart, and they wait an eternity to see each other again. Or an hour. He sighed, as he watched the hands part.

Damian sat there, gazing at the ground. Now would probably be a good time to get back to bed, but he challenged himself. He had to do this.

Stepping out of his bed onto the cold hardwood flooring in his room, the difference in temperature waking him up considerably, excitement at was he was about to do felt like electricity in the tips of his fingers.

Walking around his bedside table, he reached down, and picked up his notebook, flipping it open, not looking at the cover.

Quickly flipping to a random page, this time towards the end, thumbing through the pages before it, he stopped when he reached it and then opened the book up, allowing it to lie flat on the floor. And what he saw made him smile.

He remembered *this* clearly, the day it had happened, a Tuesday of last May, almost exactly a year ago, on the 23rd. They had walked to the park together, hands held, Cindy happily smiling, pointing out every tiny detail she found interesting, helping him explore the world around him.

They had seen a poet in the park that day, who had read to them a love poem. Damian couldn't remember the rest of the poem, nor had he written it down, but he distinctly remembered how it had started, and finished:

"The pains in loving, we don't forget
And the joys that happen, we don't regret."

This took up a tiny portion of the page, which was nearly blank. The only other thing written on the page was a tiny note jotted down in the bottom-right corner, but it was illegible.

20

He recognized the scrawl as his note-taking script, miniscule letters with the finest precautions taken to get the details right on every letter. Damian didn't spend much time wondering what he had written though – he had seen what he had wanted to see, a happy memory, and he forgot about what he had dreamt.

Momentarily freed from that dream, the memory that haunted him consistently, that he would never forget, he sat in the dark, smiling. Without a worry in the world, he spent another couple of minutes in that position, and then he stood up and got back onto his bed.

He turned his head upwards slightly to look at his clock, wondering what time it was, and how long that tiny little venture had taken him, also wondering how long he had sat on the floor, secretly savouring his memories.

The hands of the clock, separated during the time of Damian's recollections, were now reunited. This was the last thing he saw as he pulled his covers over himself again, closing his eyes, and giving himself in to sleep.

Waking up in the morning, Damian was out of bed before his father.

He pulled his curtains wide open, and sunlight splashed into his room, bathing every corner of it in warmth. Looking around, he saw his books, his jacket, and his watch.

Vague memories of the previous night still ran through his head, and the beauty of that morning brought them all back. What he would do to relive it though, was unfathomable.

Smiling again, he walked off to the bathroom, and brushed his teeth. Barely thinking about it, the only thought on his mind was of the poet that he had seen so long ago in the local park in Perten.

His community was so small; he wondered how so many wonderful people could live there: he knew each and every person on his street, all the people who worked at the plaza just 3 blocks away, and every student who attended Perten Senior High with him. This didn't actually mean that much though, when you lived in a small town, with a population of less than 2000.

Knowing everyone was pleasant, but this also meant that the people he could easily run into people he knew, everywhere he went. Every time he saw Cindy, his insides twisted, and he suddenly noticed something in the other direction that fascinated him very much. Sometimes it was a butterfly, sometimes a bird. Occasionally, it made him feel like he was losing his mind. And so, he lost his mind as he cleaned up his teeth with a mouthful of water, and started walking back to his room to get changed into some clothes to go for his run.

Damian's day blew by; in three of his four periods, note-taking occupied him, while in the fourth, his class watched a film: a movie rendition of King Lear, a tragedy, death at the hands of the insane, and guilt taking hold of those on the other end of the knife.

Quietly reciting lines under his breath, he was barely paying attention to the screen, more avidly staring at his pen, wondering if he was going to write in his notebook again.

The booming voice of Gloucester's actor resounded in Damian's ears as he recited, "I am tied to the stake, and I must stand the course." Damian was in harmony, speaking in unison with the fool Duke, and he felt himself saying the words, verbalizing his own position. Picking up his pen, he slowly wrote, scratching out words constantly, and ending with the product he expected, more or less a poem; something he had not written in such a long time.

A glance at my watch,
I see the hands,
Touching briefly,

But only for a moment,
Soon to be separated for hours,
With only a minute to meet.
One minute,
They reunite so happily,
Motionless,
Until their time is done,
And they unwillingly part,
The separation taking an eternity,
Until they meet again,
But if the watch stops,
They will be apart forever,
Stuck in time,
Never to see each other again.

After a four month long hiatus, he now looked at his prose. A fresh page awaited him tomorrow, and he smiled at the thought. This would be as close as he would get to reliving that moment from the previous night. And he smiled.

The pains in loving, he would never forget, and the joys that followed, he would never regret. He closed his notebook, putting it away in his bag.

Chapter 4

"Cindy Lau! You get up right now, or you'll be late again!"

She sighed. Her mother could be such a pain in the ass sometimes. Grumbling, she rolled out of bed... Only 8:10am? She had a good 10 minutes to get ready and then head off to school. Cindy shrugged a little *good enough for* me shrug and stood up.

Trudging over to the washroom, Cindy looked in the mirror: a mess, but that was normal, what she saw every morning anyway. Her nearly perfectly elliptical brown eyes looked so dull in the single light bulb in her washroom.

It wasn't her eyes people noticed about her though. They only noticed her slender figure, her average height, a 5'6 that looked like nothing up against Damian's 6 feet of height.

Only one person had ever made a comment on her eyes... "The colour of them, so deep: There's no way to describe them..." And that was her dorky ex-boyfriend alright. Cindy missed him sometimes... but she shook off the thought.

Running the water momentarily, she feigned brushing her teeth, quickly ran her nearly toothless comb through her thick black hair a few times and stopped to see the result.

Nothing would really help make her look better. She looked at her hair, hopelessly thick and wavy, and she knew nothing would fix it, so she refused to do anything to it. She washed it last night, and that was good enough for her. She knew she looked bad, and she took it with pride.

Running downstairs, Cindy grabbed a piece of toast and rushed out the door, grabbing her bag on the way out, almost considering leaving it at home to see her mother's reaction. A quick "bye Mom" and she was gone, dashing off to school.

Just one block away, she heard the second bell ring, and she cursed loudly. Slowing to a walk as she headed in the front doors, she stood still, vaguely paying attention to the national anthem playing on the PA system.

Perhaps three years ago, during her freshman year at Perten Senior, she might have sung along, smiling, laughing at her friends singing in different languages - but as she stood there now, outside of the front office on her 5th consecutive late day in the week, singing was the last thing she wanted to do.

"Stand on guard for thee..." and the words were barely comprehended by her sleep-deprived mind. "Please remain standing for a moment of silence." And she wondered how her life had gotten this way.

Last year was when it had started. Things had just sort of crashed and burned after she was alone.

Cindy tried to force that out of her mind though, summoning up a happy memory, to remember something from a better time. She selected a memory, and began to relive it, waiting for the morning announcements to finish.

She had been in Damian's room – she had no problem thinking of it now: the breakup had been over 3 months ago – and she had seen something out of the corner of her eye, leaning against his bedside table.

Not paying it much mind quite yet, she was busy looking at his bed, asking him how he managed to sleep on something so tiny, and starting to walk around the frame, looking for the measurement. Not finding it at the foot of the bed, she went over to the head, walked around the bedside table, and saw that the object she noticed earlier had actually been a notebook.

They talked a little while, wondering where they would go for university together, talking about a date they would go on the next weekend, the usual kind of thing, and then he hugged her, said he would be right back: he was just going to go get them some food and some drinks.

Curiosity got the better of her at that point, and she picked up his notebook, smiling gently at the front cover of it.

This picture of them, she remembered, had been taken when they had gone for a walk on the beach, in her opinion, the one beautiful place in all of Perten. The beach and the boardwalk going over it were actually just sections on a small lakeside, the other shore visible when lying down on the sand. Hunter Lake was really small... but it was beautiful all the same.

"The sun going over the horizon... haven't you always dreamed of seeing the sunset in the arms of someone special to you?... Oh, I love you so much," and he held her.

Damian was so cheesy sometimes, but she smiled either way. And they had taken the picture just like that, because they both wanted to preserve the beauty of that moment they shared: but he had clearly done a better job than her.

After picking up the book, she leafed through it, waiting for something catch her eye. Something short, that she could hopefully get through before he got back. And her gaze fell upon the first word of one of his poems: free. Quickly, she scanned through it, rushing to finish, and the whole time dreading being caught going through something he might consider to be private – even from her.

Free of all sorrows,
Rid of all fears,
Every time I hold you here is the
End to all my tears.

Cindy smiled again, wondering if this was how he felt when he was with her. It made her feel good inside, and when he returned with their food, she kissed him fully on the lips, holding on to him for a good minute or two. She felt so... inspired.

When she got home that same day, she had found herself a scrap book, and wrote their names together all over the cover. It looked beautiful to her, and she flipped open to the first page, wondering what to write. What *could* she write in here? So she decided, maybe she wouldn't write poetry, any type of writing would do, and she began writing down her feelings, what any person might expect to find in a diary. She wasn't willing to go too "out there" yet.

So, I'm finding myself writing in here... Cindy Lau, no one special, but I just felt so, so happy today. I wonder what my boyfriend would think of this if he found it. I don't think he would get mad, realizing that I saw his notebook... would he? I'm just too scared to consider the possibilities, so I'll keep this in my closet. Well, I guess life's good right now, so happy with him, I just feel so... I'm not even sure. I feel inferior to him, like he's out of my league, whenever I look into his eyes. And when he tells me I look beautiful, and I do look into his eyes, it feels so real, but it's so hard.

Believing I could possibly be beautiful and being told that by someone as perfect as him just seems so... impossible. Yet he still tried to convince me, and I smile so widely every time: but not at him, never at him. I could never bring myself to do that, and I don't think I ever will; and it just feels terrible, that I can't look at him, can't smile at him without feeling bad. I

27

just want him to know that I'm happy. Happy with him: just so, so happy with him.

I guess there's not much else to write... there's no way I could be as deep as him. I wonder if he keeps his guitar songs and his lyrics in there too... his voice is so melodic: sometimes I just wish he would pick me up in his arms and then we could run away together. The beauty of it all. Off to bed now.

That was only the beginning of things. Her entries changed, slowly, over time, until they resembled something more like what she scrawled in her notebook at around 3:00am last night:

I really don't know why I'm still writing in this every day. I don't want to have anything to do with him, his guitar, his notebook, his poetry, his voice-

What's my problem? I have to figure this out. But I know, I do want him, I just can't stand it though. I need someone to help me, to tell me... What's wrong with me? Why can't I just let him know that I'm happy? Why can I never look into his eyes? Why could I never sing back to him, show him any of my *creations, my* poems, *my* songs? *Why is he still so important to me? Someone, tell me, please.*

This had turned into some sort of a sick obsession: she couldn't go one day without writing in her notebook. And, at this moment, she realized, that over the last year, she had slowly let her heart leak out onto the pages of her notebook, and she had left it there. Left it there without realizing.

Jogging off to class, down the hallways, ignoring the waves of teachers passing by, occasionally smiling at one of the teachers she see later that day, she slipped into class without her English teacher noticing, sighing in relief. It turned out that today was her lucky day, and not the 5th consecutive day for her to be late to class this week. So she put her head down, and slept.

Damian saw that Cindy had just walked into his English class, late again, and put her head down, fast asleep in less than 10 seconds. She had probably gone to bed late last night, doing what, he was afraid to wonder.

More importantly, he still hoped that she was safe and living healthily. The relationship had just lasted too long for him to stop caring. And it pained him to care, not knowing if she did too, but he had to.

Looking away now, he redirected his mind, and thought back to what he had seen hanging out of her backpack two weeks ago: a notebook – well, more of a scrapbook.

Immediately, the first thing he noticed about the notebook was the visual layout of it. Seeing their names in conjunction all over the front, worn down as the rest of the book was, probably from use and time.

It shocked him, as he looked closer and then rubbed his eyes, just to make sure he was seeing straight. And he managed to confirm it. It really *did* seem to be a notebook of hers. But why would she still keep it with her?

That day, when Damian had gotten home, he pulled out his notebook from the shade of his bedside table and turned back to the page of his nameless acrostic that he had written less than a year ago.

Earlier the day he wrote it, he had gone over to Cindy's house, and they ran outside together. Sure, it was cold, but they had embraced afterwards, savouring each other's warmth. And he had felt so, so free.

Recalling all of this as he flipped to the poem, the page was bent downwards at the top-right corner, an obvious sign that someone had read it, opened the book, and quickly shut it down, apparently in a rush. Maybe she still cared, still thought of him.

He grimaced at the thought: no need to get his hopes up, just to have them crushed again. He wouldn't go through *that* again.

Now, looking at her peacefully sleeping through the rest of Act 5 in the movie rendition of King Lear, I wondered how she did it. How it felt to be so... imperfect, and perfect at the same time. And the bell rang.

Cindy woke up, turned, looked at me, then smiled. Blushing, she picked up her still-packed bag, and ran out of the room.

Dazed, a short dream of Damian had come to her mind, simple, yet so satisfying, but she didn't know why. She had turned, and smiled: it felt so good, almost like she was in love again. And the bell rang as she opened her eyes, saw Damian, and realized what she had done.

Quickly grabbing her heavy bag, that she never took anything out of, she ran out of the room. "Cindy!" she heard someone call out from behind her, but she didn't stop to check who it was, though she had a pretty good idea.

She couldn't look back. And she ran off, away from him, to her next period, wondering what it was exactly that kept her this way.

Sometimes, she just wished she could be free of all her sorrows.

Free.

Chapter 5

Damian was so.... confused. She had woken up, turned, smiled at him for the first time in over a year, blushed, scowled, then got up and left, all in the 2 seconds that the bell rang. Wanting to talk to her suddenly, he shouted her name, "Cindy!" and rushed out in to the hallway, disappointed by the sight that met him.

Half-heartedly, he looked down the halls, and all he could see was wave after wave of students: this was the corridor of the school with the majority of the classrooms. The other half of the schools was entirely dedicated to their sports teams; teams he had never really bothered trying to join.

In a slight daze from what had just happened, he'd thought back to what she said to him before, ending it. Her tone of voice had seemed so convincing, but not quite convicting. It didn't feel like she wanted to do it, wanted to separate herself from him, yet it still hurt when she told him they "needed" it.

"Bye Damian..." He had to talk to her.

The final bell of the day rang, and she woke up from yet another sleep session, this one in her Physics class. Why she had taken this course was beyond her, as she didn't really understand any of it. She just assumed the credit would make her feel smarter – sadly, this wasn't so.

Picking up the lone textbook she had pulled out, she put it back into her neatly arrange backpack, next to her physics notes (copied off of friends), and she dashed out the nearest doors, leading out to the back of the school, and started on her way home.

On her way out, she watched the faces of the other students in the school pass by: the others in her grade, some she knew would drop out after they graduated to go get jobs, to get married.

Others, she knew, were druggies and would fail to show up for exams after failing the course already, having to go back for another year to fail the same courses.

And some, she knew, looked down upon her, looked at her as if *she* was going to be a drop-out, a failure. And she hated it. Then she saw him. Ducking out of the crowd passing by, she walked in the opposite direction of her house, intending to go the long way – she wasn't ready to talk to him. Not yet.

After an additional 10 minutes of jogging, she had finally found her way onto her own street, her mother's section of their townhouse looking rather small now, going around the richer part of the neighbourhood to get home.

Cindy jammed her key in the door, turned it, and kicked it open, walking inside. Bending over, untying her shoes, she proceeded to throw them over to the side: it didn't seem worth her time to keep this part of the house clean anymore.

She walked upstairs, spying her mother in the kitchen on the way, and uttering a quick "Oh, hi mom, I'll help you with dinner in a few" before continuing up to her room.

She said the same thing almost every day, but she never helped. It almost made her feel bad that she failed to help her mother; maybe she would actually work today. Maybe.

Walking through the doorway of her small room, barely half the size of most of her classrooms, she felt like she had just walked into a rather large, badly decorated, cardboard box. And that was how she felt every day. Glancing around, she saw her dresser, a massive mirror, small shards broken off the sides, an unfinished composition of hers, the lyrics stopped about 4 months ago, and finally, her notebook.

Her notebook... she remembered bringing it to school two weeks ago, thinking of writing in it during her English class, knowing the teacher would probably appreciate her enthusiasm to create a literary piece during class, without the obligation to do it.

She saw him look at it though. Damian had seen it, and probably figured out what it was too. Oh... him. She almost knew how she felt now: almost ready to sort it all out. It felt right, when she thought of it now: what she thought of him was...

Stepping in the front door, he ran up to his room, nearly tripping over himself, his undone laces hanging over the edges of his shoes. Throwing them off, he continued in his rush to get to his room.

Right after entering through the doorway, he walked right to where he wanted to be.

Quickly opening the door to his closet, pushing all of his old winter jackets off to the side, he pulled it out: his mahogany, custom-crafted acoustic guitar. He had gotten it new, 3 years ago, after he had learnt how to play the Guitar Concerto in D Major, Largo, the song that had been played so long ago during his parents' wedding: his father couldn't resist buying Damian the new guitar, to make more music. Tears had come to his eyes back then.

Holding it in his hands now, the first time in 4 months, he day dreamed for a second, thinking back to the past, when he had started learning how to play guitar five years ago, how he had played his guitar for everyone to listen... and he wondered what he could do with it now.

Quickly playing a few chords, running up and down a few arpeggios, it felt good in his hands – he felt in control of something for once. Singing softly to himself, he played the beginning of the song he had tried to write, the lyrics rolling off his tongue, the chords at the tips of his fingers, until he reached that line, the line he could not finish:

> "Lying down, at night in bed,
> with you here in my arms, I said…"

Playing the last chord, a CMaj9 chord, to finish his piece with a perfect authentic cadence, he knew now, finally, what it was that he would have said 3 years ago. He would have told her that he loved her - that nothing could mean more to him.

What Cindy thought of him was that he was her lover, the person who had been at her side for so long, through everything she had encountered, through the last few years of her life. He was her Romeo, never leaving her side, ever, always willing to be there for her.

What she had tried so hard to tell him for so long, and had only thought to do now, was to tell him how she felt… she loved him.

Then, she stopped for a moment as she thought of all she had done to him: she had broken Damian's heart, left him alone for the better part of four months; she didn't know what to do. What was there left to do? And she sat there, in tears, feeling lost. What could she do?

As he played the final chord in his song, quickly jotting it down along with his completed lyrics, Damian set down his guitar, as and idea set into his mind. He had finished his song 4 months too late. Who could he play it for now? Cindy had probably moved on… and he was stuck loving her.

Sighing quietly, he sat there, motionless, the sound of his guitar still ringing through his mind – this lonely guitarist was playing in an empty stage, and he bowed, but did no one applauded.

Gazing out his window, he sighed, picked up his guitar, and lay down again, mindlessly picking away at the strings on this beautiful instrument he held now. If only she could hear him, talk to him... And this composition had no audience: it was only a lasting piece of reminiscence in his directionless heart.

Feeling lonely in a whole different way, he closed his eyes, and sang.

Chapter 6

Gingerly getting up and stretching his legs, Damian walked downstairs and out the door, shutting it gently behind him.

Bare-footed, he walked across his house's front lawn, the cool, dark green grass caressing every step he took. Once he reached it, he sat down on the transformer in front of his house, the street light above him looking downwards as he continued to play.

As he played, he peered at the time as he watched the sun set: 6:13pm. Wondering where his day had gone, and what there was to do now, he strummed away on his guitar, and she walked by him.

Instantly catching his eye, he started wondering if he had seen her somewhere before: wondered what was so familiar about her. And it just wasn't coming to him – Damian was absolutely lost. This was one girl who lived in Perten who he didn't recognize.

She sort of reminded him of the girl he had seen in Cindy when they had first dated. Full of life, but with a handle over herself: Mature, beautiful and tall, all in the same package.

She wore a white hoodie over a light pink tank top, barely showing, with her hoodie zipped up all the way in the cold night air. She wore fitted blue jeans, flared at the bottom, revealing heels, about half an inch thick.

Her hair was relatively shorter than Cindy's, maybe about a foot long, straight, and a beautiful tinge of brown, parts of it showing up as nearly jet black in the light of the disappearing sun. She looked to be Japanese, not something he saw very often around town.

Suddenly very conscious of his t-shirt and baggy jeans, he pretended not to notice this girl walking by him as he played.

Damian needed to think the situation over – had he seen her somewhere before? He swore he hadn't… and that bugged him: Perten was just too small, so seeing someone he didn't recognize unsettled him slightly.

Lost in his thoughts, he hadn't even noticed when she walked over to him, mesmerized, observing the motions of his right hand picking at the chords he formed with his left, marvelling at the smooth movements of his fingers.

"What song are you playing?" said the girl, "Did you write it yourself?" an inquiring look on her face: lips pursed together in wondering, eyes filled with curiosity, her hand perched on her hip absent-mindedly, watching him.

And he realized what song he had been playing.

He was thinking of Cindy, but watching this girl as she spoke to him: the conflict within him became torrential as he fought to sort himself out.

"Yeah… I only finished writing it recently. I could never figure out what I wanted to say – I mean, sing, at the end of the piece."

"It's a beautiful song, really it is. My name's Autumn, nice to meet you," she said, smiling.

"My name's Damian", offering his hand to her, "Nice to meet you too."

"I should probably get home soon, but… I want to ask a favour of you… Damian."

"Sure, I have the time. What is it?"

The same look on her face, full of emotion, curiosity, she asked, "Can you sing for me?"

Lying on her bed, staring at the ceiling, Cindy was still wondering what she was going to do. She knew she loved him, still loved him.... but she couldn't confront him, talk to him about it. It didn't feel right, and she just couldn't do it.

What was wrong with her? And she kept asking herself the same question over and over.

Thinking of her composition, unfinished, lying on her dresser, she wondered how she would ever finish it up.

It was intended to be a gift for him, for Damian. It hadn't just been a solo composition, merely another one of her usual piano pieces: she had written it for them, to play on their 5th year anniversary, 5 years of dating each other.

She had meant for it to be special. Her duet with him: her gently pushing on the keys of her piano, his fingers running along the smooth metal strings of his guitar. It would have been beautiful. She cried at the thought of it, how she would never be able to play her music with him again. She had to talk to him soon. *It would have been beautiful.*

Applauding for him, Autumn smiled, and he nearly fell over. A smile... so wide, beautiful: her teeth lined up imperfectly, all of her teeth in place, except her two front teeth, which were slightly larger than the rest. And, just the smile itself – he hadn't seen one for so long, at least not one directed at him. And he couldn't help but smile back.

"So, I'll see you tomorrow?" Damian questioned.

"Yes, and don't forget to call me later", pointing at the slip of paper she had left in his hand, "thank you... your voice is beautiful. Just... so beautiful."

"Erm... thanks. Yeah, I'll call you... later. See if we... have time to meet tomorrow, alright?" Flattered, nearly at a loss for words, he could barely get the words out of his mouth. "Bye... Autumn." He let her name just roll off of his tongue, and it felt wonderful.

"Bye, Damian..." she whispered, as she turned and walked away. He felt the tug at his heart. Why had he done this?

Suddenly, he felt disgusted with himself. Playing her song, the song he had written for Cindy, to another girl. He even sang it to her, vocalizing his non-existent love for her.

He just wasn't ready for something like this. Cindy... wherever she was, he needed to talk to her.

And, with Autumn's face, her body, resurfacing in his mind, he heard Cindy's voice. "Bye, Damian..."

Hunched over on the bench in the threshold of his house, he thought to himself slowly, "Why did I do that?... Why did she have to come by now of all times?... What brought me out there?..."

His head rested on one hand, the other hand keeping his guitar standing.

Sighing, he got up, deciding that too much worrying would kill him one day. He wanted to go to his room: even in his fragile mental state, Damian still wanted to take a stab at reading his own writing. He needed to.

Casually walking into his room, past the closed bathroom door, he kneeled down, and picked up his notebook, deciding he would go right back to the first page. Back to the beginning: he needed to go back to when he had started.

Cradling the spine of the book in his hands, Damian was stalling, postponing the moment he would have to open the book up to the first page, and begin to read.

Upon further investigation of the book's exterior, Damian found that the label on the back of the book remained intact over the years, and advertised that it had 560 pages, was 100% recycled, post-consumer material, and college-ruled. The cover of his notebook, outside of the photo pasted onto the front was a soft shade of yellow; one that didn't pierce his eyes as he looked at it, a sort of pleasing ochre colour.

It had seemed so beautiful, lying there on the bookshelf in the independent bookstore located in the plaza – he couldn't resist buying it, picturing the literary abandon that he would partake in, with his pen and the thick, blank notebook.

Such a long time ago, Damian thought. As he opened the notebook up to the first page, he was blown away by the amount he had written. It looked like there were thousands of words written collectively over the 3 pages he used on his first day of writing.

His tiny handwriting spoke eloquently for him, stretching from one edge of the page to the other, ignoring the margins completely.

His writing continued on and on, at first talking about how he would restrict himself to one page from that point, what he had for dinner and other trivial matters as such.

Then he found his mentions of Cindy, but that was when he had first seen her, the sentences written depicting how he visualized her perfect hair, how cute she was whenever she was talking to her friends, how she was so efficient when it came to her work.

He was love drunk, definitely, but it didn't make him feel bad in any way. He felt good that there was a time in his life when he felt okay with expressing that, to a piece of paper, exposing every thought that came to mind.

As Damian mouthed Cindy's name one last time, he then forced himself to redirect his focus to other elements of his entries.

His eyes wide open, surveying the page, he flipped back to the beginning of his entry, and marvelling at what his handwriting looked like back then, before note-taking and the relevance of speed over precision took over. Quantity over quality.

Refocusing on his writing, it looked as if he had taken the time to carve each letter into the page, putting in an extensive amount of time and effort: which he probably had, as he was so excited to break into his newly purchased notebook, a fresh blank canvas, with his literary art.

He finished reading all his writing from his first day using the notebook, and began reading the final sentences over again, slowly, wondering what he thought of them:

> ... and then my dad told me that there was no way that he would let me date someone until I was out of high school, but I think I'm just going to ignore him. I saw her yesterday, and I had a nice conversation with her. It was a bit short, but I still loved talking to her: she's just so happy, every few seconds flipping her hair back over her head. Beautiful, just so beautiful. I wonder if she'd go out with me. She seems kind of... out of my league, I guess they'd say. I can't wait to see her tomorrow, but until then, I'll keep thinking of what to say. I want to get to know her better.
>
> Au revoir, et à demain,
>
> Damian Huong

Realization dawned on him, as he understood that he was correct earlier. This was what he had seen in Cindy, what he saw in Autumn during their brief meeting.

Considering that, he'd have to get to know her better, in fact, yes, he *wanted* to get to know her better. She was definitely out of his league, but he still had to try. What to do about Cindy... he didn't know.

It felt so wrong to him though. He couldn't just leave Cindy, with all that they'd been through. He couldn't go for Autumn: that wasn't an option for him.

Thinking about how he would excuse himself from meeting Autumn tomorrow, and calling her later tonight: perhaps just call her tonight, cancelling for tomorrow, and saying he couldn't talk for long because he was busy would work.

It made him feel bad for making plans and cancelling the night before – and as he thought of this, his eyes fell, yet again, upon his composition, finished in the light of his distress: Autumn Fantasies, that's what he would call it. Just a fantasy, it wasn't real. He still needed to talk to Cindy and sort things out.

And he heard the Cmaj9 chord ring through his head, each note pronounced clearly, and the end: harmonized with everything that preceded it.

Chapter 7

Cindy had just finished dinner, and was now perched on her bed, lying down and facing out the window of her bedroom. It was 6:25pm according to the alarm on her bedside table: the sun still in the process of setting, a violet ray of light lining the horizon now, the outside world barely visible now, the silhouettes of various objects engulfing others.

What she could see clearly out the window was a girl walking away from Damian's house, smiling - the type of girl who made Cindy feel conscious about herself: this girl wore her confidence all over her body and face.

Getting her mind off this girl though, and how elated she seemed to be, walking home so late, she looked over at her duet.

She had added a repeat earlier, to take her back to the chorus one last time, but with an alternate ending. The ending would be slower than the rest of the song; it also featured a calling and answering between the piano and the guitar, finishing with a beautifully harmonized chord.

She debated for a second, and decided on a Cmaj9 for both instruments to end on. The strings on the guitar, and the strings struck within the piano in unison would sound consonant together – but this, she only theorized. There was no guitar for her to sample the piece with.

The whole piece would be blindly based on what little knowledge she had in how a guitar and piano sounded together.

And she frowned slightly, rolling the thought around in her mind. She was the piano; at most times she would be *estinto*, nearly lifeless in her piece, not audible over the feature of the stronger, dominant chords from him.

He was the guitar, *energico*, full of life, his arpeggios rising and falling melodically in front of her countermelody, a wonderful contrast to her light finger strokes on the white keys.

Her pencil on the paper, scratching in a few chord symbols, verifying the harmony between the two instruments, the numbers and letters all over the page made her feel slightly better. She knew how to do this, and how to do it well. Some hope rose up in her, and she made up her mind.

She would speak to him tomorrow, just start a normal conversation, stay off the topic of what had happened months ago, perhaps ignoring the fact that it even happened. And one day, she would hear her piece, share it with the world: Relentless Reminiscence.

Playing the chorus to herself softly, sitting on her piano bench, she was overtaken with feeling, and couldn't bear it. She stopped, closed the lid on her old piano, also closing her eyes, and running her hands along the wooden finish. It was glossy, regularly dusted off, smooth to her touch.

Her fingers felt bare, not entwined with his, not running through his hair. She felt the weight of her composition in her hands, hoping to, once again, feel complete.

Resting his guitar against his bedside table, a light shadow cast over his notebook, it looked right, the set up of his belongings seemingly perfect in the truncated light, and so, he smiled, but only for a second.

Picking up the phone from his work table, he dialled the cell phone number written on the scrap of paper he had taken out of his wallet, put there earlier, after Autumn had rounded the block.

The bland tone ringing in his ear, he anticipated the moment she would pick up her phone. His mouth going dry, suddenly forgetting everything he was planning on saying, he gulped.

"Hello?" She picked up on the third ring.

"Umm... Hey. Yeah... this is Damian. I'm a bit busy right now. I don't think I can... um. Talk. For long." His words were all tied together, refusing to leave his mouth in one piece, and his sentences were awkwardly punctuated.

"Oh! Hey! So, how about tomorrow?" She just sounded so happy... how was he going to do this?

"Well, I think I'm busy. I have some... studying to do. And, I want to finish writing another song that I started on the other day." Yes, just build on something that she knew about: that sounded convincing. "Maybe next week?"

"Oh..." she sounded disconcerted, "Alright then. I'll see you some other time. Are you sure you're..."

"Yes. I want to finish off high school with good grades, you know. Maybe I can play the song for you when I finish it, alright?" It hurt him, to have to let her go, before getting to know her at all. The bite in his tone refused to soften up though.

"Okay then... I'll talk to you tomorrow? Call me if you're not busy. Good luck with your –"

"Wait! Two days from now, Sunday, I can see you. We'll meet down at the beach at 2:00pm, alright?" So much for letting her go. "I'll bring my guitar too."

"Awesome! See you then. Have fun with your studying. I know your song will be wonderful. Goodbye, Damian."

"Bye, Autumn." Her name – it felt too good on his tongue. And he hung up.

Holding the phone, Cindy's fingers hovered over the keys. She wondered if she was actually going to call him. No, this could wait until after the weekend – and she set the phone down in its base again.

Beginning to walk away from the phone towards her living room, maybe to sink into her sofa, to melt into the cushions, watch some television, it rang. Rushing back to it, she picked it up and pressed "talk", still recovering from the shock of it ringing.

"Hello, who is this?"

"Erm, hey. Do you have a few minutes?..." It was him. It was him!

"Definitely. What's up?" She was shivering with excitement. He had called her! Then again, there was the problem of what she was going to say, but, still. He called her!

"Do you have plans for tomorrow?"

"I don't think I –"

"If you don't, I'd love it if we could meet. George's Café in the plaza. At 2 in the afternoon. Maybe for an hour or so, we could talk. Does that sound good?... If not, we can reschedule."

"No, no. That sounds wonderful. I'll see you then?"

"Yeah. Alright then. Nice to talk to you again, Cindy. See you."

"Awesome. Tomorrow at – " *click*.

Though she had just been hung up on, she was just about ready to jump through the roof; she was just so excited to see him again tomorrow.

Running up to her room, she had already begun to think of what she would wear tomorrow, what new clothes she had to match with the ones he used to love her wearing. Then, it came to her, the clothes that he had loved on his girlfriend – that was not who she was, not anymore.

Still, she was ecstatic as she picked out the most innocent outfit she could find, not wanting to provoke him in any way, she felt it was a tiny bit too modest to wear to see someone who she felt for like she did for Damian. The outfit she planned on choosing was more like something she would wear to work, but she had to play it safe. Didn't want to dress too flashy and scare him away.

She inhaled deeply, and exhaled as calmly as she could while hopping up and down on the spot, shifting her weight from one foot to the other. She couldn't stay still, not until she ran out of things to prepare for tomorrow, at which point, she could walk away from the closet.

The rummaging didn't take all that long though, as she sorted through tops, pants, looking for any sort of clothes that she deemed appropriate to wear for Damian the next day.

Finally finished, she climbed into her bed, the time barely 10:00pm, she went to sleep quickly, smiling as she closed her eyes, she was in for peaceful sleep for the first time in 4 months.

Chapter 8

Casually sitting at the table in George's café, they faced each other, his feet flat on the ground, her legs crossed tightly — signs each of them recognized on the other, of being nervous.

"Well, how have you been doing?" Damian asked Cindy, with a hint of concern. He was trying to keep the mood light, so that they might drift onto the topic of what had happened. Their break up, 4 months ago.

"Okay, I guess. Exams coming up, prepping lots. How about you? How're you doing?" she replied, seemingly over-excited.

He looked at the way she was dressed. These were what she wore to work, to see people she was unfamiliar with. Did that mean that she wanted to be further from him? That she only show up today as a consideration to him?

"Every chance I get. Just cramming in as much stuff as I can, you know? I swear, I've read King Lear at least 5 times in the last 2 weeks alone. Almost no time for guitar now..." No need to mention Autumn. Not now, not when he wanted Cindy, wanted to talk to her, to get to know her again.

"I know exactly how that feels, but... I just have a question for you..."

"Sure, what is it?" He was worried now. Cindy's eyes were wide open, her left eyebrow rose as she watched him respond. It was sort of strange: that was the look she wore when she was very upset with him, but wanted to hide it.

"Who is *she*?" she spat out, as he turned around, and saw Autumn there, holding him, running her hands through his hair, whispering in his ear, "I love you, Damian…"

Sweat running down his back now, Damian woke up and sat up in his bed in the dark. That was definitely a new dream – and not one he enjoyed in the slightest.

Looking around him, feeling extremely insecure in that moment, he looked outside the window: the world outside of his room was also pitch black, except for the tiny halos of light generated by the few streetlights that managed to turn on every night.

Intending on getting back to sleep soon, he rolled over, placed his feet on the cold, hardwood flooring now, and he stood up.

Damian walked down the stairs, into his kitchen, flicked on a light and poured himself a glass of cold water. His mouth had gone dry, the opposite of what it was usually like when he woke up, and he was pretty sure his throat was sore too.

Standing in the dim light of the only light bulb that would turn on in his kitchen, staring around, he gulped down his water, thinking of his meeting that would take place with Cindy in a few hours when he woke up again. "Who is *she*?" He considered the possibilities of what might happen during their meeting.

Feeling the last drop slide off the cool glass onto his tongue, he set down the empty glass on the counter, and walked back up to his room, hand on the railing, up the spiralling staircase in the central area of his home.

Looking up, nearly reaching the top landing of the staircase, he peered through the skylight, the new moon refusing to stare back down at him, to light up the night world for him. It was just a closed eye, high up in the sky, yet another one that wouldn't look into his. He felt tired.

Finally making his way through the doorway to his room, he re-arranged his blankets, flipped over his pillow, and lay back down on the firm surface of his mattress.

Spinal health was one of his main concerns ever since his father had managed to injure himself lifting their old furniture out of the house, and Damian had convinced his father to get him a new mattress after that point.

This mattress had lasted him a good 3 years, and still seemed to be in good condition.

Resting his head on the pillow, closing his eyes, he hoped to fit in some more sleep before waking up again, to the sight of the sun.

If he looked terrible tomorrow when he saw Cindy again, what would that do for him? With Cindy on his mind, and thoughts of Autumn surfacing at regular intervals, he eventually managed to fall asleep.

Damian's alarm rang, waking him up, and he pounded his hand down on it. 8:30am, reasonably late for him, in comparison to his usual time to wake up on the weekdays, and he climbed out of bed, feeling slightly better after his nightmare.

Taking off his undershirt and putting on a clean t-shirt, a plain black one, he applied his deodorant as he walked out to the hallway, and into the bathroom.

Shutting the door behind him, he set the deodorant stick down in his cupboard, and took out his tooth brush, tooth paste, and comb. He came out of the washroom a full 30 minutes later, looking better than he usually did, his hair raised and hovering over his forehead, his face clean, looking alive for once.

Nearly skipping, he headed back into his bed room and threw his closet doors wide open. *What is there to wear in here, that wouldn't become too sentimental, or suggest informality?*

Rummaging through his tops, the metal coat hangers scraping against the horizontal pole they were suspended on, he eventually just pulled out a blazer, to wear over the black t-shirt he had put on earlier.

This was the type of clothes he usually wore with his friends, but not a jacket she had seen him wear before. He hoped it was slightly cool outside, so he wouldn't burn up in it though.

Taking only a second to debate on the topic, he just pulled on a pair of his old black jeans. He decided they would go well with what else he was wearing, and the only decent pair of shoes he had right now, some black runners, with matching black laces and a design in gray streaked across the sides. They really did look better than they sounded whenever he described them to anyone.

Damian felt prepared as he walked down the stairs, looking at the kitchen clock as he opened up his fridge, pulling out a pair of eggs and the carton of orange juice: 9:10am now.

Setting these objects down on the table, he grabbed himself a bowl, a glass, and a frying pan.

Setting the stove on high and placing the pan on the oven, he cracked the eggs quickly, landing them in the bowl, and began stirring them with a pair of chopsticks he left on the counter yesterday. They seemed clean enough.

He beat the eggs, mixed in some salt, and poured them onto the pan, a satisfying sizzling sound occurring now, music to his ears, and his hungry stomach.

Poking them in the pan, effectively scrambling the yolk and the whites over the flat surface, they seemed nearly cooked after only a minute of poking and moving, so he turned off the stove, and poured his eggs onto a plate.

They looked delicious, as he put some black pepper on them: this was the only way he would eat them.

Sitting down at the table now, his meal before him, he poured himself a glass of orange juice and put the carton back into the fridge.

Ravenous, he dug in, devouring his entire breakfast in barely 5 minutes, again thankful that no one was there to watch him eating.

As he wiped his mouth, he stood up and placed the dishes in the sink – he would wash them later, when he came back from his lunch date with Cindy.

Scheduled for 2:00pm, he hoped to be back from it by 3:00pm. That would give him plenty of time to wash the dishes and then ease into his room before his father came home from seeing his colleagues in the bar by the beach.

Walking into his living room, he began to pack everything he planned to bring with him to lunch into a messenger bag: his composition, some lip balm, a mirror, his comb, his keys, his wallet and his notebook. These were objects he felt insecure and incomplete without.

Draping the bag over his back, he walked out of the house, locking the door on his way out, he decided to walk down to the plaza right away – being a bit early would give him time to walk around, and then wait in the café for her. He had never kept her waiting before, had never been late for a date with her, and he wouldn't start now.

Sure, she knew that the date with Damian was at 2:00pm (thinking of it as a date got her just that much more excited for it), but Cindy had still woken up at 8:00am for reasons unknown to herself.

Normally, she would sleep in on a weekend, perhaps until noon, to make up for all her lost hours during the week, but she felt strangely energized as she jumped out of bed that Saturday, and she skipped over to the washroom.

Staring into the mirror, prepared to tame her hair, she picked up her brush, and ran it through a few times, to no avail. Cindy decided that she would just take a shower: it was such a simple solution to such a tedious problem that would take her forever to solve using other methods.

Quickly slipping back into her room, Cindy grabbed the clothes she was planning on wearing today, an outfit meticulously planned over several hours the previous night. It consisted of a white dress shirt, and a tan/beige long skirt, reaching her knees: she left it all on the bathroom counter as she undressed and stepped into the shower.

About half an hour later, she stepped out, condensation everywhere, all over her mirrors, the glass of the shower stall, some on the ceiling – and she felt so warm, wonderfully comfortable in her skin.

Drying herself off, and putting on her clothes, she walked back to her room to grab her straightener, which she never used, to be used in conjunction with the hair dryer she also never used. Her hair had never seemed to matter as much as now, when she had a reason to look decent.

Stepping back into the washroom, patiently working down each section of her hair, she watched herself, and she saw herself as she did over a year ago, before her school work began to bury her. This was what she looked like after exams last year: this was the time when she was willing to accept anything that a guy said about her being beautiful. *It felt wonderful.*

Now rummaging through her cupboards, she took out some light eye liner, and found a small pair of earrings – modest, nothing too much.

Putting both of these on, the eye liner and earrings, she smiled, gave her look a try, and smiled wider as she realized how much she really liked the way she looked when she spent so much time on herself. Still, too much work for her.

Why did it have to take so much to make herself look pretty? Then she thought about what Damian had said about her and simplicity, "Your features are more apparent when you're not wearing so much make up, the shape of your lips, your face, they look so perfect on you; you really don't need to dress yourself up to look beautiful, Cindy." Always making her want to smile, but she had never been able to. And she frowned.

Checking the time, 10:00am, she walked downstairs, hearing her mother in the kitchen, working the stove and cooking breakfast, she greeted her mother.

"Good morning Mom!"

"Oh, you're finally done. Goodness, you never take that long in the washroom. I thought you'd passed out in there. You're up early today Cindy... Anyway, sit down: breakfast is almost done, and it'll be warm for once. You always wake up so late, I swear your breakfasts have always been cold. I made us eggs and some toast... Wait, are you going somewhere today?" Her mother raised her eyebrows, turning around after her absent-minded breakfast talk, her attention now set upon her dressed up daughter, not looking like a wreck for once on a weekend.

"Yup! Going out to meet a friend later today at George's Café. We're just going out for lunch, don't worry – I'll be back in time for dinner," Cindy replied, addressing her mother's only worry every time she said she would be out for the day. And she really would be back for dinner this time.

Cindy thanked her mother as her mother set eggs and toast in front of her.

"Alright then, have fun. Call me if you need anything... you know I'll be at Charlotte's mom's house, right?"

"Of course I remember, you told me last night." Something vague was coming back to her mind. Her mother had probably actually mentioned it. "Don't worry."

"Alright. Finish your breakfast, then wash the dishes, I have to leave early to get there. They live on the other side of town now, you know? They moved into the house of that strange couple who moved out a few months ago. Such a big house too... pretty. I'm going over to see it today. I heard they have neighbours who just moved in too!" That meant her mother would probably be back barely in time for dinner too.

"Cool. Have fun then," Cindy told her mother nonchalantly.

Spooning eggs into her mouth and chewing off chunks of toast, she was amazed that her mother hadn't complained about her talking with her mouth full yet. Clearly her mother's mind was somewhere else, exploring the large house across Perten she was about to visit.

After a few more minutes of eating in silence, her mother got up, put her dishes in the sink and ran some water over them. "Don't forget to –"

"I know. See you later!" And Cindy waved at her mother as she began towards the door, her purple summer dress, a floral pattern all over it swaying with her steps. She pulled her purse over her shoulders and closed the door, a final "Bye" as she locked the door, leaving Cindy alone at the table.

Finishing the last bite of her breakfast, Cindy joyfully strode over to the sink, placing her dishes lightly on top of her mother's, picking up the sponge as she turned on the tap.

Pouring some dishwashing liquid onto the sponge, she suddenly wondered how other families managed to use a dishwasher to wash their dishes: it took so much longer, was so much louder, used so much more money... how lazy could you get?

Running the sponge over every portion of the dishes that she could reach, and then scrubbing over those spots again, she set each dish into the other sink as she made her way through the small pile.

Nice to talk to you again, Cindy. See you. His voice, still the same, with that melodious ring to it, stuck in her mind, hypnotically dragging her through the chore of having to wash the dishes that morning.

She couldn't wait to see him, but was still nervous, the encounter only hours away. What if she messed up? What if something she wasn't expecting happened later? Why *had* he suddenly decided to meet her for lunch?

Chapter 9

Reaching the plaza, the sun was beginning to shine brightly, rising higher up into the sky. Damian took off his jacket and decided he'd put it on later, in the air conditioned café, when the time came. *Goodness, it's really hot today*, he thought to himself. Wandering around aimlessly in the open parking lot, he noticed a few cars he recognized parked in front of the breakfast restaurant; he was pretty sure the family who owned those cars had said they were leaving to Vancouver for the summer, and they were going to leave two weeks early. Catching breakfast before leaving, he guessed.

Damian walked past those cars, both spacious vans, and made his way into the bookstore – he hadn't shopped there for personal reasons in... 3 years and 10 months, give or take a week.

Every purchase he had made more recently than that had been made out of the textbook shipments the bookstore received for Perten Senior High, or a legible version of the Shakespeare text that his class was required to read for the semester – the tattered old copies the school loaned out beginning to get on his nerves.

But, 3 years and 10 months ago... he remembered when he spotted that notebook on the shelf, and he sighed, clearly in for a trip down Memory Lane, he stepped away from that particular shelf.

Browsing the other shelves in the store now, currently popular novels that he had never heard of in any context other than in correspondence to a new movie to be released in the theatre in the centre of town were all he could see.

Built right next to the church and a buffet restaurant, the theatre was a rather small one, with only four big screens, in four rooms, excluding the main hallway. Though it *was* small, it remained a popular spot for the teenagers in this area, and the theatre managed to make excellent business, even in the small town of Perten.

Back to rummaging through books he found on the shelves, nothing caught his eye: reading for pleasure just didn't seem so appealing anymore. Engulfing himself in the literary works of others had always excited him, the opportunities to read yet another person's story, to live yet another person's life.

That worked well for him, rendering excitement from reading fictional pieces, but Shakespeare happened the moment he had gotten into high school in 9th grade, and he had then leaned on writing his own pieces. Reading non-fictional works and absorbing knowledge suddenly became more gratifying than fiction, and his old reading habits had been torn apart.

Reaching the end of the Fiction and Literature section, he stopped, turned around, and walked back down along the book shelf, reaching the end in a few seconds.

Damian left the book store, gently pushing the door open, a light jingling sound accompanying the movement, the bells on the door shaking, announcing his departure.

Back out in the hot summer air, Damian took a deep breath in, and walked away from the book store. Cindy had a knack of getting to places early, usually by about an hour, so he decided he'd get to the café as soon as he could, 2 hours before scheduled.

He really didn't want to keep her waiting at all, and he wanted to do it quickly and get it over with, but also take his time. Obviously, he hadn't thought it through very well.

Opening the door to the café, he waved at George Terranova, the manager and owner of the café. On his way in, he sat down at his and Cindy's favourite table, the metal chair scraping as he pulled it out from under the table. The table was located in a corner of the café, opposite the washroom, and beside the largest window of the shop, offering a beautiful view of the rest of the plaza, and offering people in the plaza a wonderful view of whoever occupied those seats. It still felt amazing to be sitting next to such a tremendously large window, top to bottom, from one side of the shop to the other, though, and that was why they always sat there. It let them feel like they were eating outside, with the feel of eating inside, a perfect balance in ambience, setting the mood for whatever they were to discuss on their dates in the café – he still remembered that at least.

Damian pushed his chair in a bit, closer to the table, as he looked around at the décor of the café: it was the same now as it was 5 years ago when he first went there, with a few very minor changes over time. The lamps hanging above remained the same, simple, the paintings hanging all over the walls – unidentifiably abstract and "modern". Underneath these paintings, George had purchased large varieties of potted plants for further decoration, a natural aspect to add to the simplicity of the design of his café.

Checking his watch, the arms slightly hazed by the heat of the outside, it looked to be about 12:10pm: he had quite a bit of waiting to do. He took off his jacket and hung it on the back of his chair, setting his bag down on his lap and opening it up.

Rummaging through the bag, he extracted his notebook, and opened it up to a random page – this was his plan as to how he would kill time being so early to meet Cindy at the café.

Damian wanted to keep her on his mind, maybe plan what he wanted to say to her, which, being quite honest with himself, he hadn't thought of yet. All he knew was that he had to fix things, and soon. He needed to get his feelings back under control... he needed to get Cindy back in his life.

Lost in thought, Damian was brought back to the real world abruptly as George called out his name, "Hey, Damian! Can I get you something...?"

"No, it's alright. I'm waiting for Cindy." Might as well talk to *someone* about it, and seeing as she would show up soon anyway, in perhaps half an hour, he could just as easily pass the time talking to George.

"You two get back together or something?..." So he had figured out they broke up. And Damian wasn't surprised by this at all: after the break up, he had stopped showing up to the café on a regular basis, only passing by and waving at George through the giant window, watching the young, 30-going-on-31 year old Italian man stop washing the dishes, or rearranging the chairs, and wave back at him.

"No... not yet, I guess. Just talking to her right now, you know?" He *hoped* George knew, because he sure didn't.

"Oh, I see. Alright then, I'll get you guys the usual when she shows up?" A vanilla latte with chocolate sprinkles on top for him, and a decaf cherry mocha for her, more mocha, less cherry.

"Sounds great. Thanks George."

"Nice to see you back here, kiddo. I missed seeing you two in here every week... good luck, alright?" said George, as he walked back into the back of the café, probably already preparing for the rush of customers at night, washing and drying the last of the dishes, pulling out his stock of alcoholic beverages.

"Thanks..." mumbled Damian, too quiet for George to hear as he disappeared through the door. A sign bearing the words "Employees Only" hung on it, though everyone knew very well that the only person who worked in this café was George himself.

Sighing, Damian picked up his notebook again, flipping back to the page he was intending on reading before, and explored his writing. The piece he opened up to was written September 7th, right before the beginning of the school year, after he had begun dating Cindy during the summer, three years ago. This slightly longer poem, written in prose, was titled "Gaze":

> Looking into your eyes,
> Searching for your heart,
> And wondering if it is truly there,
> If what you show me is this,
> Is the vessel of emotion that hides within you.
> The steady pulse,
> All these lies, constantly circulating,
> Running under your skin,
> Through your veins,
> Throbbing in your mind,
> Released now, upon me.
> I see them, hear them,
> *Believe* them,
> And as I watch all your blood,
> Your lies,
> Rushing through you,
> I wonder where you have kept your heart,
> Deep inside of you,
> Hidden away from me,
> Where no one can see it.
> Sighing, I continue to search,
> Determined that some day,
> I'll find it, your heart,
> Looking into your eyes.

Upon finishing the poem, he was confused as to where the idea for it came from, so long ago, just like all his other ones... it seemed more like what he was feeling right now. He was looking for her heart, through her eyes, but he couldn't see it. He couldn't even see her eyes. Not her smile. Nothing. So, how he was expected to find her heart, to love her fully, he didn't know, but he still tried; still tried to search for Cindy's heart. And that was what he was doing now, today, sitting in this café, waiting for –

The door of the café opened, Cindy already looking at him as she entered, smiling widely, beautiful in her skirt, a light blue colour that matched the colour of the summer sky that day. Her hair flowed downwards, slightly past her shoulders, floating through the air with each step she took. Noticing she took time to dress up for their date, he felt relieved: she cared, to some extent, about how she displayed herself for him, leaving some sort of window of hope open for him.

Suddenly, he realized he was still holding his notebook, and he scooped up his bag, and shoved the notebook into its depths to be hidden from Cindy's eyes, hopefully before she questioned it. She watched this motion - him hurriedly hiding away his notebook - and she only kept smiling at him; she already knew what it was that he put away in his bag. Warmth radiated off of her as she looked him in the eye and smiled her polite smile: perfect.

Sitting down, she decided she would start the conversation, "Well... you're here early, aren't you?" she asked, in a light mocking tone.

"Can't hurt to be early to see you." One of the oldest lines he had used while they were dating. "Great to see you, Cindy. You look wonderful today," Damian said.

He hoped his tone didn't make it seem like he was getting overly sentimental with her.

"Thanks. The same goes for you. Umm... how long have you been waiting for me here?" She looked a little concerned, as well as a little guilty, making him wait for her – she had done that every single time she showed up early, to find that he had already arrived earlier - and he had already prepared his response: this was just the way it used to be.

"Oh, not too long, don't worry. Exams coming up, I brought some of my notes to study off of anyway. Killed some time in here... the place hasn't changed at all, hm?" Clearly treading in dangerous water speaking about the past, and things changing, he was almost absolutely sure he was going to regret saying this in a few very short moments.

But he remembered how she reacted to him talking like he used to, and how she had just smiled at him. Things would probably be okay.

"I agree... this place is still just as beautiful as before... it always feels great being here." She wanted to add "with you" so badly it was painful for her just thinking about it. Cindy sighed lightly, fiddling with her hands on top of the table.

Suddenly, they both turned and faced the counter as George stepped out of the back room with their drinks, already made, though neither of them had actually ordered yet. Setting the frothing latte in front of Damian, and the small mocha in front of Cindy, he returned to the back room, winking at Damian on the way, "Enjoy!"

"I haven't had this in so long... oh goodness..." And tears started forming in her eyes, as she held her drink. Something about seeing the steaming hot beverage in front of her seemed to pull and tug at her heart.

For once in her eloquent lifetime, she felt like she couldn't find the words to explain what she felt.

"I miss you, so much... I don't want to keep going on without you. Please... I think we should try again."

63

"Cindy... don't cry... I know what you mean. We've been apart a little while, and... I think I feel the same way. We'll try again. Will you... go out with me, Cindy?" His thoughts were a rapid swirl in his mind right now... he couldn't think straight. The only thing he knew at this point was this moment, here and now. He loved her, and he needed her back in his life.

"Yes... that would be wonderful, Damian. I... I love you. I'm sorry I couldn't tell you that before" said Cindy, her eyes blurred through her tears. The small droplets pounded against the surface of their table, yet she looked so happy.

Damian held her hand, and smiled to himself lightly. Finally, he felt whole again, but, what could he do about Autumn? He chased that thought away - he didn't need to think of it quite yet.

Sitting in silence following their sudden outbursts, the quiet was only interrupted by the occasional sounds of sipping, cups being set on the surface of the table, and George working in the background.

They were together again.

Occasionally meeting eyes, smiling, they drank their beverages, slowly working their way through the afternoon, in the cool, air-conditioned café, hands touching on top of the table.

Eventually, at around 2:40pm, Cindy excused herself from the table, picking up her bag as she stood up, "I need to go use the washroom. I'll be right back." And she disappeared into the female restroom.

Watching the last few strands of her hair flit through the air, seemingly about to get caught as the door closed behind her, Damian thought to himself about what he had done.

He had closed his window of opportunity with Autumn, had refused himself the chance to get to know her, and now he was dating again.

Yes, he was happy, but at the same time, it tore him apart from the inside – *what if*'s kept flying through his mind, though he tried not to let them ruin his happiness. He had to realize, he loved Cindy, and wanted to be with *her*.

But, did he?

Standing in the washroom, she set down her bag on a dry part of the countertop: though public washrooms always disgusted her, she felt better about George's Café's. He constantly sanitized the area, as he was just about as much a germophobe as she was.

Opening her bag, she reached in and took out a napkin, wet it under the sink, and wiped her face clean. Her make up had begun to run down her face, making her look like an absolute mess. After another minute of cleaning herself up, she felt she looked acceptable.

Cindy ran her hands under the facet, the warm water and soap bringing a light aroma to her nose, and she let her thoughts run wild.

She had been saved the trouble, and he had asked her out again, and she had said *yes*.

She smiled, knowing her life could probably return to normal: she would work so much harder to try to keep the relationship working, to keep her life in order, to make it into the university they wanted to go to together.

Again, she did a small check-up of herself in the mirror, admiring the happiness she found on her face that she couldn't find before.

No matter how long she looked though, she couldn't find what Damian saw in her, and how he could keep calling her pretty. It was unfathomable.

Finished with cleaning herself up, she walked back out to the café, sitting back down at the table with Damian.

Checking the time, it was already 2:03pm. Smiling to herself, she thought of how meeting him so early had made their date at George's Café finish a few minutes after it was scheduled to begin. Funny, how they still knew each other well enough to show up so early.

Damian watched Cindy as she walked back to the table and said to her, "I just paid for our drinks. Why don't we go outside and walk for a little? Unless you need to get back home…?"

"No, it's fine. I have time to spare. Let's go," she replied, smiling. They were going on a date, the first one in 4 months.

As they left the café, she felt beautiful again as she looked into his eyes, and got lost in them, melting away at the sight of him, Damian, her boyfriend, her rescuer. *Her lover*.

Chapter 10

There's Autumn, sitting in the park... on our bench.
"Cindy, how about we go down to the beach?" he said, attempting to avoid a potential commotion. He was afraid of what he would have to do, already happy at finally solving the problems that arose before: his emotions, his break up with Cindy, everything.

"Why?... It's such a nice day out, and the park isn't that full... we'll have a lot of space to walk around, to talk," she replied, looking slightly confused, a slight frown forming on her face.

"I want to see the beach again... You know when we took that picture 3 years ago? On the boardwalk?" he asked, pulling every thought that came to his mind out of his mouth in the form of an excuse, attempting to jog some memories, distracting Cindy as quickly as possible.

He didn't want everything to just crash and burn.

Upon hearing this, her face brightened, and she began to smile again, her pace slowing, and responding, "That would be wonderful. I'm pretty sure my mom wouldn't mind if I stayed out late, actually, now that I think of it. An extra hour or two won't kill me."

"Cool. We'll go to the beach then. Relax a bit by the lake, so we can cool off. It'll probably work wonders for my studying later, either way." He felt relieved, as he would be heading away from the park, away from his "Autumn Fantasies."

Which reminded him.

"Cindy, when we get to the beach, I have something I want to show you, and I'm pretty sure you'll like it," he told her, smiling.

It was 5:14pm as Cindy inserted the key to her house into the lock on the front door, and turned it. With her hand on the doorknob, she kissed Damian goodbye, waving happily at him as he turned to get ready to walk the three blocks back to his house. "Good night, Damian. Thank you..."

"Good night, Cindy. Bye... I'll talk to you tomorrow. If you come by, we can probably study together," he told her, barely suppressing a wink as he did so.

"Yeah, I should probably start studying... right... exams begin, what... 3 weeks from today?" she asked, though she wasn't really worried about them. The concern about her academic success hadn't quite sunken in yet.

"No, actually, 2 weeks. Don't worry, just drop by and we'll study together. I'll help you study for your Economics exam too," he offered, always the hint of concern in his voice.

"Awesome. Well... I love you. See you tomorrow, Damian," Cindy said, beginning to shift towards the door.

"I love you too. Tomorrow, around 2:00pm?" he asked, beginning to sound worried she wasn't taking exams seriously. He jokingly wondered to himself if she would actually study, while she was over, just because he told her to. 2:00pm: that was the time they planned to meet each other, all the time, anywhere they went, unless it was absolutely impossible to make that time for whatever they were doing.

"Sounds great. Bye, Damian," she said his name again, the ring of those three syllables sounding so wonderful in his ears.

"Bye," he said to her for the last time that night, kissing her on the cheek quickly, once, before taking his first step away from her house.

Walking in the front door, she was met by the smell of dinner - a strong seasoned chicken, probably in a dish with some sort of Chinese vegetables - and the sound of her mother walking around the kitchen, cleaning up whatever she needed to.

Cindy could tell that her mother had only recently finished cooking their dinner though: there was the sound of the oven's vent running, but no sound of the oven still operating, or the sound of food being fried on the pan, probably now sitting in the sink.

"Hey Mom! Sorry I'm a bit late... I got caught up. I was out today with Damian," she informed her mother, hoping to get some sort of response, to have her mother question her actions, to start a conversation.

But her mother didn't take the cue.

"That's nice. Sit down, dinner's almost ready. Get yourself a bowl, and get yourself some noodles. The meat should be cut in about one more minute. If you're too hungry, there are some leftovers from the rice last night," her mother told her as her mother absent-mindedly poked the chicken, flipping it over, constantly checking if it was burnt in any spots, cutting off anything she didn't feel she would eat.

Cindy walked over to the cabinet and grabbed herself a large bowl, suddenly conscious of how hungry she was. She walked over to the drawers, grabbed herself a spoon and some chopsticks, and then sat down at the dinner table, beginning to shovel food into her bowl.

Later, as the bowls were being washed by her mother, Cindy thanked her, and ran up to her own room, suddenly feeling really tired, though it was barely 7:00pm.

That day was probably the most active day she'd had since… well, she couldn't really remember.

Tired, she sat down by her table, and picked up her composition, "Relentless Reminiscence" hoping to run it through, if not on her piano, then at least in her head.

Staring off into space, she could hear the melody playing peacefully, the guitar accompaniment harmonious to the soft sound of the keys of the piano in her mind. The ringing sound of the strings within the piano being struck, gentler than the guitar's plucking, but still harsh… she just couldn't get the image clear in her mind. She needed Damian, but the piece wasn't finished yet.

In 5 days, it would officially be four years since they had begun dating, and she wanted this piece done for him on that day, so they could play it together.

She thought back to earlier that day – he seemed to be hurrying to the beach when he walked away from the park.

She remembered thinking, *There has to be a logical explanation behind this… there has to be something that he just* can't *wait for*, and she had been correct.

The moment they got near the beach, they stopped just outside the sand, in a cool, shaded, grassy area, under a tree with a picnic table for them to sit on.

This time, unlike the confrontation they had across their table at George's, they sat next to each other.

Damian set his jacket down on the table, then his bag on top of it, opening the bag up, and pulling out a few sheets of paper that looked in great condition, as if he protected those papers specifically.

They seemed important to him.

It turned out that *Damian* had written a song for *her*, with lyrics and all, on those pieces of paper. He would play it for her the next day when she went over to his house to study; she couldn't wait to hear his voice, singing to her again. She knew that he didn't sing for anyone else, ever.

Smiling, she got back to fixing the melody of her song, making minor notes here and there, extending chords where she felt necessary, sharpening or flattening notes at every corner of the piece.

She wanted everything perfect for the 20th, the coming Friday. *Four years.*

As Damian walked back home in the dark, he reached deep into his bag, fiddling around and pushing everything aside, wondering where his keys could have gone. Two minutes into searching, his hands finally made contact with the cold metal teeth of his copy of the house key, and he dragged it out of the endless pit he liked to call his bag, and used it to open the door.

It really wasn't that dark outside, the time only being about 6:00pm, but it was dark enough that he couldn't see clearly, which made him feel blind and insecure enough.

Rushing through the door, Damian locked it quickly after slamming it on the way in, knowing his dad wasn't home.

He rushed into the kitchen, grabbed a piece of toast, and ran upstairs.

Jumping into the chair in front of his work table, he picked up a piece of empty sheet music, and dove into his newest composition. This one, he wanted to prepare for their 4th year anniversary, which, in all technicalities, would be the coming Friday, five days from then: June 20th.

Thinking back to earlier that day, he wondered what had driven all of it, what it was that had gotten him through the entire day. Hour after hour of self-conflict, over Cindy, over Autumn... life could get so confusing.

Then again... he still had plans with Autumn the next day by the beach when school cut out. He'd call her at that time and cancel – he didn't really feel like caring about anyone but Cindy at that moment, sitting at his desk, pen poised over the paper.

Turning around... he looked at his notebook, catching a glimpse of the cover, and a small smile formed. He would share his poetry, all of it, with Cindy that Friday: she'd like it, hopefully, along with his new song.

And so, Damian scratched down at the top of the page, as the title of his new piece, "Fresh Beginning", probably soon to change, but that was dependent on him.

This would be a lighter piece, entirely instrumental, so he could focus on articulating his notes fully, and producing the beautiful sound he wanted.

He wanted... no, *needed* to sweep her off her feet with his music. And so, he began with the ending of the last composition, as he thought was only appropriate... the first chord of his piece that would soon lead into the first verse, a simple riff, based on a minor scale with a sharpened 6th, was a Cmaj9: the

end of his Autumn Fantasies.

Chapter 11

In the front doors of the school at the time he usually got there in the morning, about half an hour before the first bell rang to inform everyone that the day was soon to begin, he saw someone who wasn't usually waiting for him in the group, standing with the rest of his friends.

Speeding up his stride, he quickly closed the distance remaining between Cindy and himself, then, suppressing a grin, he took her into his arms. He couldn't help but notice at this point that she looked a lot... what was the word? Happier, at that time. She just seemed to shine like the Sun, standing next to him, even if she was indoors. It just made her so much more beautiful, contrasted against the dull grey walls of Perten Senior High's interior.

After a few seconds in a tight embrace with her, Damian finally let go, cuing Cindy to do the same.

They held hands as they walked out the front door again towards the bleachers outside of Perten Senior. The bleachers were right on the edge of the school's track, which was yet again bordered their massive fitness rooms.

Cindy and Damian both sat down on the benches, silently joined by their hands, not really knowing what to say until Damian broke the silence, facing Cindy and stating more than asking, "Nice morning out isn't it?"

And it was. The sun already high up in the sky, the day was warm, but not terribly humid. Not at that point anyway. "Did you sleep well last night?" Damian continued to inquire.

Looking back at him, Cindy replied, "Yeah... the clouds are so puffy, and perfectly shaped. They remind me of, um... marshmallows? I'm not really sure. But they're pretty anyway. And, last night, I slept wonderfully," though she looked tired, "I was working on... something, late last night. I need to get it finished for this Friday."

"Oh, your Independent Study Project?... Is it for English?" he guessed, but she shook her head to both of his questions. Damian was left wondering what she could have possibly been doing. "Erm, what is it?"

"Just a little... actually, yeah. It was my project... thing," she told him, though she looked off into the distance as if she was trying to avoid telling him something. *What* was *she doing last night that kept her up so late?*

"Alright then," he replied, respecting her privacy, but still pondering what she did.

There didn't seem to be anything else to say.

Again, they sat in silence, but it wasn't an awkward silence, or a cold one. They were merely a couple of people who sat side by side on the bleachers, staring out into the sky, waiting for a new day to come, to sweep them through the journey of time. And, finally, they would be able to make that journey together.

Fifteen minutes after the final bell had rung, after the majority of the students in the school had fled the interior upon dismissal, they sat on the benches outside of the school. Damian and Cindy, holding hands like they were in the morning, were the only ones remaining in that general area of the school grounds.

Checking the time briefly, 2:45pm, Damian said to Cindy, "Why don't we go over to my house now? I can help you study for exams... you realize they're coming up really soon, right?"

"Oh... I know. Thanks. I really don't think I can pass with a studying and work ethic like mine. Just let me go home and get changed first, alright? I'll get to your house as soon as possible. I shouldn't take more than 20 minutes... sound good?"

"Yeah, sounds good," he replied to her, as she got up and began to walk towards her house. He really thought he should walk her right up to her door, but whenever she announced that she was going to go back to her house before going somewhere with him, he knew she wanted to be alone.

Sighing, he walked back to his house one slow step at a time, but still reached his house before Cindy reached hers.

He unlocked the door and stepped inside, throwing aside his shoes in the usual manner, but suddenly remembering Cindy was coming over, and instead, put them up on the shelf. He didn't want to look bad on the first time she came over again.

On his way into the kitchen, hoping to grab something to eat quickly, perhaps a slice of bread or a fruit of some sort, Damian came across his father sitting at the table, drinking coffee and reading a newspaper.

"Oh, hey there Dad... umm... do you mind if I have Cindy over today?" Damian inquired, slightly worrying about what his dad's response would be.

"Erm... sure. Does she want to stay for dinner?" It seemed like his dad didn't care all too much about the situation.

"Depends how long we take to study. Thanks Dad. She'll be over in about 20 minutes, alright? Don't worry, I'll answer the door." Something seemed wrong though... his dad wasn't normally like that. His behaviour was strangely passive, as if his mind was somewhere else completely, and though it felt awkward, Damian decided he'd do the right thing, and ask.

"Dad… is there something wrong? You seem kind of, erm… I don't know." It was more awkward than he remembered speaking to his dad about how he felt: his dad had never been the kind of person he felt he wanted to go to for anything related to emotions.

His dad maintained a stiff look, his facial expression frozen in place, nearly emotionless, and he brought the newspaper up in front of his face slowly, feigning sudden interest in another article in the newspaper. Attempting to pass off the info he was conveying to Damian now as any piece of news - not that important - he spoke again, his voice not quite as even as his expression, "The Chan's… they got into an accident. All three of them, Mrs. Chan, Mr. Chan… little Nicholas. A really bad accident too: it was on the highway, a drunken truck driver…"

It seemed his dad couldn't hold it in any longer as he set down the newspaper and began groping blindly for the tissue box that he knew was somewhere on the table. Damian passed him a tissue, and his dad muttered some form of gratitude. After a short bout of tear-wiping and nose-blowing, he continued, "Young family… The parents… they weren't even 35 yet, and their kid – he was in your grade wasn't he? Only 17, he hadn't even turned 18 this year. They're all dead. All of them. I can't believe it…" and his father dissolved into tears again.

Seeing his dad so vulnerable suddenly made him feel self-conscious of his imposed presence, but he also felt obliged to stay. If he left, it would feel terrible, just having his dad lying down on the kitchen table, gripping the newspaper tightly, tears running down his face.

After a few more minutes of staying in the kitchen to no effect, to Damian's disappointment, it didn't seem like there was anything he could do for his dad at that point. He sighed.

Before leaving to head up to his room, he pushed the box of tissues up to the space directly in front of his dad. He'd be able to help himself from there.

Making his way into his bedroom and sitting on his bed, he wondered how anyone human, anyone with a heart, with feelings, could consider their own problems so large. A break up, a rejection, some change in feelings... those were nothing in comparison to facing death. Death was the end, no return from it, and it broke people who were still alive, taunting them, torturing them. The loss of a close friend, a loved one... the fear of their own ends coming soon, or what it might be like when it met them. Sitting there, right then, he could feel Death staring at him right in the eye, refusing to blink. So he closed his eyes, lying down in his bed.

Damian couldn't take it anymore... this area so commonly had drunk drivers going through that there were cops on borders just for that purpose: to keep them out of the city, and protect the citizens.

Sadly, this didn't mean that it was free of them, and every once in a while... he didn't want to think about it anymore.

Cindy had finished changing into some nice clothes: an ever-so-slightly less modest skirt of a dangerous black colour, along with a white blouse contrasted against her bottom half. Though there *was* a desire to look nice for Damian, she wanted to appear presentable in case Damian's father was home. Making a final check of herself in the full-length mirror in her room, she was satisfied and left her house, beginning to walk off to Damian's.

Reaching the door, she paused for a moment to check a compact mirror she kept in her purse to make sure, yet again, that she looked fine. It was almost as if she was checking if something had ravaged her face over the few blocks it had taken her to walk to Damian's house. Relocating loose strands of her hair and applying lipstick one final time, she held out her hand, and rang the doorbell.

Head in his hands, he was thinking of death, how it was everywhere now… no, it always *was* everywhere, a ubiquitous presence in his life, looming over people he knew, ruining their lives. Nicholas Chan… always innocent, obedient to his parents to an extent that every parent partially wished their child was more like him, he wanted to go to Harvard, had plans to go, had been accepted in fact.

Kind of annoying at some times, but, Damian remembered when they had been kids, growing up together in Elegant Fern Public School… they had been best friends, sharing cars, crayons: anything that they trusted the other with, which was nearly everything a 1st grader could get their hands on.

Later on, in Fedora Heights Middle School, they had, yet again, been best friends. At this point, puberty was the big thing: who was getting girlfriends, who still had voices comparable to pre-pubescent girls… oh, so much teasing, he could remember.

Going into Perten Senior High… things had been different. He didn't want to be around his "best bud, Nick" so much anymore, and he forgot why. But he would never forget Nicholas. He exhaled deeply.

And the doorbell rang.

Dashing down the stairs, not wanting his dad to get up and answer in his place, he reached the door in a matter of seconds and wrenched it open, greeting Cindy with a quick kiss on the cheek. Leading her inside, he announced to his dad, "Dad! Cindy's here, alright?"

Momentarily, there was a faint reply of "Okay!" muffled heavily by the sound of tissues and the two went upstairs to Damian's room, closing the door behind them, only leaving it slightly ajar so that his dad wouldn't come barging in wondering what was going on.

To her, his room probably looked more or less the same as it had four months prior. She was just looking around, sitting on his bed, searching for some sort of difference in his tiny room, but as far as she knew, it was exactly the same place she had been before, which it was.

On his way over to his closet to pick up his guitar and English notes, he took his new composition from the top of his desk and stuffed it into one of its drawers, not wanting Cindy to see it before it was ready.

After retrieving what he went looking for, he walked back over to the bed, sat next to Cindy and handed her his notes.

Pulling a highlighter out from the pencil case he kept under his bed, where he kept his extra writing utensils. He patiently skimmed through, highlighting the key points of the entire play, King Lear, and told her that she should focus on those parts. As he highlighted, she watched him curiously, her head tilted slightly to the left, watching him at work.

When she took the book from him, he watched her reading through, her lips moving silently, her eyes darting across the page... he wanted to paint the moment, to capture it in a frame, on a canvas. That would be magnificent.

Running both his hands along the strings quickly, getting a feel for the thin metal wires, he began warming up and humming notes harmonically to the chords he was playing to stretch his fingers. Just for the heck of it, he sang some lines out of King Lear to the tune of his guitar, just to get a smile out of Cindy, to make her laugh, calm down, and be able to study stress-free. About to begin singing the first song he wrote for her, he was stopped by his dad yelling for him.

"What is it?" Damian yelled back at his dad, truly wondering what his dad could possibly want with him.

Pausing for a second, his dad yelled back, "The phone! It's for you!"

Chapter 12

Damian rushed down the stairs, slowing down before reaching his dad – his mind was stricken with panic: who could call him right now, or at all, other than…

His dad handed over the phone, questioning Damian in the process, eyebrows raised. "Who is this? It's some girl who's asking where you are. Says you told her you'd meet her somewhere."

Not looking in his dad's eyes and not responding to the question either, he put the phone to his ear, not wanting to get into the awkward moment where he would have to explain that he wasn't cheating on Cindy yet. He had a feeling that's what his dad was concerned about. Speaking in a quiet, meek voice, as if he might dissolve into the floor if he tried hard enough, Damian finally spoke, saying, "Hello? Autumn?..." He hoped she had given up, had become impatient, unwilling to wait, and that would be the end of things.

"Damian? Is it you?... Where are you right now? Didn't you say you'd be at the beach right now?" Darned caller's ID when he called Autumn to change their plans beforehand. He'd basically handed her his phone number – *goodness*. He felt ridiculously stupid in that moment, thinking the hundreds of better ways he might've chosen to do things that wouldn't have ended with her calling him. He would even go as far as to say she was stalking him.

"Sorry, I'm really busy right now. Way too much studying that I have to do for exams coming up... I tried to call you, but you never answered the phone." Excuses were pouring out of his mouth, words blending into each other, his mind clouding over. At that point, an image formed in his mind, of himself, at the beach, still single, with his guitar... singing to Autumn. Shaking the thought off, he tuned back in and continued listening to the phone, and to what Autumn had to say.

"- so, yeah... I guess... alright then. We'll just see each other some other time then? You're really sure that –"

"Yes, I'm really sorry, okay? Some other time, I promise." And when he hung up on Autumn, cutting her off abruptly as she despondently replied goodbye, he thought: *there's another promise broken.*

Ignoring his dad's hand held out to take the phone back from him, Damian entered Autumn's phone number in to the "blocked callers" list of their house's telecommunications system, crossing his fingers mentally in the process that she would give up and not call him again anyway.

Once he was finished, he handed the phone back to his dad – the look on Damian's face blatantly showed his annoyance at the surprise call, calming his dad down considerably. The concern that showed on his dad's face previously - probably more for Cindy, who he liked quite a bit, than for Damian - disappeared in that moment as his dad took the phone back from him.

Running up the stairs, he slowed to a walk and entered his room quietly, to see Cindy with Autumn Fantasies in her hands, looking the piece over with interest. Damian was glad that he kept the meaning of the title to himself, only thinking of its meaning in his mind, refusing to notate what his title meant anywhere. What Cindy was looking over might as well have been just another untitled piece: as far as she knew there was no meaning behind it.

She was humming the melody of the second verse to herself, eyes closed, not even noticing his return to the room.

As Damian walked behind her, slowly, finally standing right over her, Cindy opened her eyes and turned around, smiling shyly at him and saying, "Oh... you know, I really like this song... But what was that all about? Who was looking for you?"

"It was John, don't worry. John Sutherland, in English. He was asking about what key points there were to study in Act 5, so I just told him that I would let him use that page of my notes next weekend," Damian said to Cindy without missing a beat.

"Oh... cool. That reminds me... I think we should start studying now... my mom wants me to get home by 6, so we have a good two hours to break this all down and look over your notes. You realize that it might be a little hard to bring me up to the point at which I won't fail this exam?" she questioned, rather, stated to him, doubtfully.

"I do realize that... and therefore, I'll just consider this a challenge, and one I must partake in to fulfill myself. That was about the gist of it, I guess. This'll be fun," he smiled, laughing slightly at his overly haughty first statement, and at how he was referring to studying as fun in front of Cindy.

"Well, sure, but we'd really better start now, and get digging through all of this..." she said, looking in disbelief at the masses of notes he had made over the last semester.

"But where to start?" Damian inquired dramatically, setting his guitar down in a corner of his room as he did so.

After he put his guitar down, Damian walked back over to his bed and sat next to Cindy again, putting his arm around her. A Fresh Beginning.

Holding her cell phone in disbelief, she vaguely noticed the time: 3:34pm. Normally, she would laugh, thinking of how close the time was to 3:33pm. Oh, three of the same number when she looked at the time, always enough to put a smile on her face, the small, quirky things in life. Conversely, she felt like tossing her cell phone at the ground... but she resisted the urge.

Autumn Kizuno, in her graduating year at Forest Peninsula Senior High, was never really allowed to feel normal - and never in her life, had she gotten as close as then. The boys at her school, a private school, were too interested in books, cars when you found a quasi-normal one, and more books. If one dated a girl, they would go for the girl who knew the most about what they knew about, the girl who was most interested in the things they were interested in. It almost looked like they were hunting for a female version of themselves to date. It was sad really, the way she looked at things.

She remembered, two weeks prior on Thursday, walking home from school feeling worse than usual, she had been turned down by a boy she had had her eyes on for the past few months of the school year, Jimmy Wu. In fact, Jimmy had been an object of her interest ever since the beginning of 11th grade – that was how long she had wanted him, ever so slightly, in the back of her mind. And then, she knew what it was like to be turned down, then, she found out what it was like to relive the experience... with Damian.

She walked away from the beach, not wanting to think back to the dreams she had the previous night, thinking of meeting Damian there... Damian Huong. She didn't want to think of having him play his guitar for her, having him sing to her, the beach empty, a private show, and spending the evening together, slowly falling in love with each other. Fruitless dreams.

Love, always a secret interest and desire to her, wanting to be like every other girl in the neighbourhood, all of them dating except her, she wondered why she could never get anyone to feel for *her*. Every time she got anywhere near dating, her parents would find out and find some sort of way to contact the boy themselves and kill off all contact between that boy and their daughter.

Still holding her cell phone in her hand, staring at its closed lid as she sat down on a bench near the beach, under the shade of a healthy willow tree, she wondered what she had done to make Damian not show up. He *had* told her that he had to study for exams, but, for some reason, that didn't seem like the entire reason behind why he couldn't meet her.

She was almost absolutely sure that he had shown genuine interest in her... until he hung up on her. Later that night, she had debated calling him back, but decided against it. No point in trying again when he would just use the same excuse, and not contact her any further, out of annoyance.

Frowning, she felt the tears welling up in her eyes, but she refused to let them out, to release them, those raindrops filled with emotion, and let them hit the ground.

She merely sat there, on the bench, feeling the cool ocean breeze, wondering if she would ever find love.

They had just begun flipping through his notes on Act 5 for the second time when both of them had begun to feel tired, neither person really feeling like studying any more. But, for Cindy's sake, they were obliged to continue. She sat more upright, suddenly conscious of her posture, and grabbed the first page of his notes, made about 4 months previously, and read over the little comments made on the introductory speech of their professor, for the third time.

"Oh my goodness! I can't do this anymore!" Cindy stated rather loudly, expressing her frustration at the amount of material she had to go over and cram into her mind for an exam that would only last a total of two hours. Then again, her mark depended on it.

"We haven't even started looking at testable material in depth yet. Okay, how about we just skip ahead, past the introductory stuff from February, and begin to look at this... here we go, my analysis of the first passage in Act I. I really hope you read that at least, the actual play, or else I don't understand how you got through this entire semester without the prof screaming at you," he said to her, shaking his head as he did so. There was genuine surprise in the tone of voice he used to address his thoughts on Cindy's survival of the last semester, as he was really amazed by how she had done it.

"Nope, I haven't read it, not one word of the entire play," she told him, as Damian picked up the play text and set it down in front of her, so she could read it over. Picking it up and looking at it sideways, observing the thickness of it, she asked him, yet again not believing the amount she needed to go through, "Are you serious? This thing is the freaking Bible of Shakespeare, isn't it? This is really just one play?"

"Not quite... but, yeah, that's all King Lear. This'll take you a while to read over. Just look over Act 1, Scene 1 right now, and then you can look at my notes on it after, so you can fully understand what you're reading," Damian told Cindy. She looked unconfident in what she would be able to do, so he attempted to reassure her, saying, "We'll work through each and every scene like that, taking it slowly, so don't worry. No need to rush. We can pull this off before exams roll around."

"I can't freaking believe this..." Cindy muttered in reply, as she opened King Lear text and began reading, her eyes hazing over at about the point she should have been at the fourth word of the play. Damian could tell his task wasn't going to be easy, but he'd have to make it happen for her.

Standing up for a moment, he stretched his arms, yawned, and walked over to his work table, picking up New Beginning again to look it over. Cindy had probably read over it more times than he had at that point, seeing as she kept scrutinizing every note he had written ever since he had shown it to her earlier that day. She hadn't made any changes to his musical piece, not even one, but he suddenly had the feeling of intense attentiveness to his piece, and how it was structured. Why was it that she kept reading over his piece? Had he made some sort of harmonic mistake? Had he done something wrong with the rhythmic patterns? Or did she want to hear it? Whatever it might have been, he thought he had a pretty good idea of it...

Listening to Cindy mutter lines out loud repeatedly back and forth with herself, attempting to find the point of emphasis in the lines, identifying the meter in Shakespeare's writing, Damian thought of his own literary works contained within his song. There were his lyrics, branded along the tops of all the staves in his song, "Lying down, at night in bed under a new / moon, with you here in my arms, I said...I love you."

Reading his own lyrics again, he turned around to look at the girl who was sitting on his bed right at that moment, and called out her name, catching her attention. Breaking her out of the Old English trance she was trapped in, he declared to her, "I love you, Cindy."

Chapter 13

With slightly less than two hours remaining for them to study, Cindy had successfully finish reading over Act 1, Scene 1 of King Lear. She had also managed to finish reading over Damian's notes on the scene, confusing herself in the process.

Damian set his finger down on an acronym he used in his notes, pushing Cindy's hair out of her face and tucking a few loose strands behind her ear with his other hand, and began explaining to her, "I used this to notate lines that showed character traits..." then he pointed at the text he had scrawled beside ever appearance of the acronym, and said, "and these are the character traits being shown, along with historical figures they're similar to, as well as people in power current-day.

Damian watched her sigh: Cindy clearly wasn't thinking of anything as she stared at the book mindlessly, other than giving up on the useless project of finding aid in her studying, and just leaving herself to fail. Damian took this in to account, then hugged her and squeezed her lightly. "Alright – we'll take a short break. Do you want a drink?" he asked her.

"Yes! I'd love one. Thanks, Damian. Just a glass of water would be excellent," Cindy replied to him, with an emphatically sweet smile on her face. She was just so cute when she grinned widely like she did, dimples and teeth showing, the smile reaching all the way up to her eyes... he couldn't get enough of it.

"Alright. We'll take 15 minutes off. Give me a few minutes and I can get us some snacks or something else to eat too. Be right back," he told her, just as he turned around and walked out the door and down the stairs.

Damian flew down the stairs, taking them two at a time, only slowing down on the last bend to jump down the last five steps; he walked into the kitchen, this time without any interrogation from his father, and took two glasses out of the cupboard.

Setting the glasses down on the table nearest the fridge, he walked over to the other side of the kitchen. After opening the cupboard attached to the wall on that side, he pulled out a dish. Setting the dish next to the glasses, Damian set off on his journey to find the cookies.

Finally, she would be able to close her eyes and rest. Still sitting on the bench by the beach, Autumn's tears had stopped falling, and she could once again focus on the calm beating of the water against the jagged rocks further off-shore, the sounds of the wind blowing by her, the trees rustling in the breeze... the world became beautiful again, and she felt she could look at it the way she usually did, always looking for the good things, seeing past the bad.

Calmly lying down on the bench, Autumn felt the warm sunlight on her face, in her eyes, on her lips, and she became impassive to her surroundings, refusing to think of the hurtful thoughts she contained in her mind and just focussing on the world around her.

So, in her state of serenity, she thought back to her childhood, and even more recently to just a few years back. She though of how she had done this before, taking on a calm indifference to the troubles of her life, and just giving in to nature, and the beauty of life.

The warm darkness she was captured in with her eyes shut freed her from her body for just a moment, the calm sounds inside and around her surrounding her, the chatter of other people on the beach becoming only a vague thought. The salty ocean air reaching her nose, she began on an olfactory stroll down memory lane...

When she was a child, she had lived in Tokyo, her family's house located on the shore of the Tokyo Bay, their property worth hundreds of thousands of dollars. Whenever she was home, it was with both of her parents, or neither of them. Her parents worked together making business deals, so they weren't apart very much. So, when she wanted something, she couldn't just ask one, she would have to ask both, and no matter what, one would deny her of what she wanted, and the other would have to agree. That was why she never asked for anything from her parents unless she absolutely needed to. She had been trained to know she wouldn't get what she wanted.

Every day after she finished school and was dismissed, before going home and walking in her front door - at which point her parents would force her to practice on her piano, or practice making her handwriting neater - she would walk down to the shore of the bay and lie down for a few minutes, just to get away from her stressful world. The waters washing in and out from the ocean in that bay, the waters were clean, and their beauty was hers: only hers, every time that she visited them. It was the one thing she could desire and get, by herself.

Abruptly, the sound of a seagull calling from above her brought her back to Perten, whisking her out of Tokyo, away from her memories and back into the present.

They had moved there a little less than a year previously and had still barely settled into their spacious house on the West side of Perten. That was the side opposite the plaza with the cute little café she had passed by the day when she had walked down Maple Valley Road and seen... well, she lived a far way off from that side of Perten.

The area where she lived, everyone owned larger houses... in fact, her neighbour had the largest house in all of Perten apparently, and had moved there quite recently, but she had found out they had only moved from another part of Perten into that house. The city was so small, yet still beautiful... and the beach – well, the beach was just a tiny piece of her old home in Tokyo that she was able to find in her new home.

Autumn sat back up on the bench, feeling she was done with her reminiscence. She ran her hand over her face, the exhaustion of getting up early that day for school and anticipation of her meeting with Damian all day had started to set in. She was feeling the smooth texture of her skin, the defined features of her visage, but she couldn't believe it was her face she was feeling – it was more like it was her mother's face she was touching. Where had the time gone? Though she wondered, she was not willing to go into another bout of recollection, so she set down her bag and opened it.

Out of her school bag, she pulled out her sketch pad, glitter all over the front, her name inscribed in the bottom left corner with her favourite pen: she had gotten the sketch pad in Tokyo, and she, always being nostalgic person she was, kept every one of her belongings she could that held memories of the past. In that sketch pad, she regularly, though not daily, drew whatever she was compelled to draw.

She opened it up, flipping past pictures of flowers, anonymous faces of people she did not know, various depictions of abstract scenery, to a fresh page, smoothing it out as she looked into the depths and possibilities of it. Autumn still remembered the first day she drew in her sketch pad, she had thought nothing in the world could be more intimidating than a blank page. Being honest with herself, she still felt the same way, every single time she tried to draw something she hadn't drawn before. It was unexplored terrain, uncharted waters, *something new.*

Unzipping her pencil case and soon brandishing her black pen in her left hand, she began to draw, forming lines that could be hair, or could be grass, ambiguous and ubiquitous, ever-present on the page before her. Continuing, refusing to add more detail, the lines continued to form an image, though she still did not know what it was, and no visible contour of what she was imagining was forming on the paper before her. That didn't deter her though, and she continued to draw, wondering what would happen.

Eventually, she came to the point where she saw a forested scene in her originally abstracted black lines, and felt her concealed feelings tugging at her heart, knowing something inside of her was becoming apparent, trying to speak. She stopped, and lifted the pen off the paper, marvelling at the beauty of the trees, the perfect contour of the grass on the page. Then, with the use of the same black pen that created the scene, she set it all on fire, bold, elongated strokes burning up the picture, flashing across the page, setting it alight.

Sitting on Damian's ridiculously small bed in his room, Cindy was attempting to make the most of her break from studying for her English exam. The horrors that awaited her in the next two weeks were apparent, but that really didn't make her want to prepare herself for them any more than she wanted to before.

She rubbed her slightly sore eyes, tired from staring at and analyzing a single scene for the last half hour or so, and she knew what she wanted to do now, waiting for Damian to come back upstairs.

Cindy walked over, around Damian's bedside table, and then picked up his notebook gently, going through to the most recent page, apparently an entry from a mere two days ealier, and she read, the guilt of reading through her boyfriend's writing only an indistinct contemplation. The piece, titled "Obscured", was written in a very thick script, meaning he had probably pressed very hard on the page, or used a really leaky pen:

> Dim candlelight,
> Shining through the darkness,
> Barely breaking through,
> But still visible,
> Offering sight to all around it.
>
> A small glimpse of hope,
> And I see where to go,
> What do with myself,
> Only a peek,
> At the future of my life.
>
> And as I walk,
> Toward this dim candlelight,
> It is extinguished,
> Smothered along with my hopes,
> Throwing me back in the dark.

Re-reading the last sentence before she began closing the notebook, quickly setting it back down beside Damian's table, she wondered what his hopes had been in, and where those hopes had gone… it felt like everything was her fault - that everything was because of her.

She thought back to what the darkness was like for *her*, and then what it was like when her candle had been re-ignited. The four months of her time, lost, and spent away from Damian… she didn't want to think of that span of time again. She still blamed everything on herself… not being able to show

Damian her feelings, and breaking down, just being miserable, for months.

She continued thinking, even as Damian walked in, smiling with what looked like a ridiculous sensation of success, that everything was all her fault.

She knew she wasn't required to carry the burden of everything that happened, but it would take her shoulders a while to stop trying.

"I'm baaaack!" said Damian, announcing his entrance, just as he saw Cindy sitting on his bed, staring blankly at the floor, then up at him. "Is something wrong, sweetie?"

"No, nothing's wrong. I was just thinking about... you know... us being apart before... and all of that. It was just on my mind, nothing important. Nothing to worry about, alright?" she replied to his question, though there was clearly a problem, stress showing on her face. "I'm so sorry, Damian..."

"Don't be. There's nothing that you need to apologize to me for... really, nothing. We'll add another 15 minutes to the break then. Studying can wait. Here's your water... and, want some cookies?" he asked her, holding out the dish of cookies. Sure, he wanted to comfort her, and he really would have if he known how... but those moments were always just too awkward for him.

He felt that couldn't do anything about it, and she knew that, but she felt comforted anyway. Those four months didn't need to mean anything – they were the same couple they were before the break up, and nothing really changed. He held her hand, and she rested her head on his shoulder.

Autumn checked her watch casually, and saw the time, along with the sun, still high up in the sky: it was only 4:12pm. It seemed like she had all the time in the world, and as she stared at the razed forest she drew, she knew that that was the only part of her life she had control over: her pen and her drawings.

The forest, healthy grass growing, bending slightly in the wind, the hundred-year old trees sprouting upwards, reaching towards the heavens and perhaps containing animals that had their homes there for decades: she had taken her power over her drawing, and set the scene ablaze. The fire of black ink trailed across the entire page, effectively detailed enough to simulate complete destruction of the forest, but not thick enough to cover up the beauty that the scene originally consisted of: the fine details in the tree trunks, each blade of grass a single pen stroke. She was the only person in the world who was able to do this to her drawings. *She had control.*

The thought made her curious though... she had no control over her life, unless she was holding a pen and referring to a sketch pad as her life. And she *still* couldn't find love, not even when she had control. Such a strange situation, to have complete control over something but still not be able to find what she wanted... but that just made her wonder what it would be like to draw love for herself; what it would be like to have control of that?

Then there was another problem: what would love look like as a picture? What shape did love take when put on paper? These questions remained in her mind as she tried to identify what love was, the unfamiliar emotion that she had never been allowed to feel. The question stumped her: what *was* love?

The shape of a heart came to mind, a child's arts and crafts shape, but that was too cliché, too generic for her liking... there was also the idea of a smile - but how to put that into picture format, and have the viewer discern between the image of love and of happiness? Love and happiness... they almost seemed synonymous, though, she knew that to many others, they were nearly opposites.

No appropriate material symbolization of love came to her mind, and she ran empty of concepts very quickly, a sudden deficiency in her imagination occurring.

Staring off into the sky, the sun only beginning to arc downwards into the horizon, the amount of light she assumed she had left would give her a good hour or so to stay outside on the beach. She could keep wondering how she might be able to apply an image to love, to fathom the question that had never concerned her so much before then.

It began getting colder soon afterwards though, the sun's heat not reaching her completely anymore as day shifted into night, and she thought to herself at that moment: to draw love, she would have to feel it.

Chapter 14

Cindy's watch beeped lightly, interrupting the couple's intense scrutiny of Damian's musical piece, him with his guitar in hand, her with a pen raised over the paper.

Every suggestion they decided on, to change a note's piitch, to modify some articulation marking to another, Damian would test it first, and they would compare the sound of the new note to the old one. At that point, doing English was only a vague memory – Cindy didn't really care: she'd get a passing mark regardless, even without studying.

"It's five now… You're really sure you don't want to do any more studying?" Damian asked her with concern. Clearly, he wasn't overjoyed with the thought of her only getting slightly above 50 on her exam, when it was within his power to prevent it from happening.

"English is just a mandatory course I've had to take for the last four years in high school. On the other hand, music has always been, and will always be, my life," she said to him, her voice filled with meaning: she was both thinking back to her past - her learning how to play piano - and declaring the path of her future, as she spoke.

Cindy was thinking of a career path in music. She always talked about it, and Damian was absolutely sure she'd be excellent at it. Cindy already had plenty of background knowledge in music, and she had such a passion for it – and with that combination in attributes, it was the perfect profession for her.

Himself on the other hand... well, he knew he loved chemistry; really, he always had, since he was introduced to the subject in 9th grade. His interest of chemistry weighed against his love of writing and playing music - this all had him fighting with himself on the inside: what was he going to do after he graduated that year?

Sure, he did have an application accepted to Grey Falls Institute of Applied Sciences, the same university where Cindy was going. Everyone he knew was already congratulating him on planning on double majoring Music and Chemistry, but he still didn't feel the pulling and nudging in his heart of really *wanting* to do something with his life. His dad would never allow him to write songs for a living, to play his guitar for money – his dreams were worthless to everyone. Everyone except Cindy.

"I know, Cindy," he said, in response to her vocalization of how she felt about English as a course. Then they got back to his piece.

"Do you think it would be better if I used a chord here in the supertonic degree of the piece, or if I kept the sub-dominant chord?", Damian asked.

The two of them got back to working on, and taking apart, Damian's composition, the one he had originally written for Cindy, Autumn Fantasies. Though the title *did* refer to Damian's little secret, he kept it that way, and for all either of them knew, it was still Cindy's song, and only Cindy's.

Cindy's mind continued to grind away, thinking of possible substitutes for everything: notes, rhythms, and chords, while Damian worked his fingers up and down the fret board on his acoustic Epiphone Elitist model. With his guitar, he brought each change in the music to life, handing full musical power to

Cindy, so that she had absolutely everything she needed to work. The expression on her face the whole hour they continued working was one of ease and enjoyment, as she re-engineered his piece.

Damian, sitting next to her, watched her, and he knew why he loved her, in that moment: beautifully frozen in time, intently staring at his composition, she sculpted his Autumn Fantasies around herself, showing him what she said wasn't a lie.

Music was, and always would be, her entire life.

And he fit right in.

The sun really beginning to set, the world around her slowly becoming darker and darker, Autumn noted the time was well past 6:00pm.

She needed to get home soon or else her parents would be furious, so, she packed up her sketch book and her favourite pen, and began to walk towards the other side of town, back to her home. By the time she got there, it would actually be night time, and therefore, it was best that she left earlier.

In Perten, there were barely any streetlights, and the city of Perten was tossed into near complete darkness at night. It gave her the chance to see the stars each night, something she was never able to do before, in the busy region of Tokyo, where the world was still wide awake all through the night, lights shining everywhere and blocking out her view of the sky.

She didn't want to go home though: she would have to play piano for whatever guests were over, help her mother with cooking dinner for that night, study for exams, and basically, for the most part, just be put back into the real world. She hated reality. And exams.

Either way, she would have to get home. Putting her left foot in front, then her right, she eventually found her way home, a reasonable amount of light still out. The dark let the night sky light up for her, but it still scared her. With the Sun just finishing it's fall across the sky, the clouds all in marvellous blends of dark purples and greys, there was still enough light that she didn't feel terrified, insecure, or lost. That was good enough for her.

Standing on her empty porch, taking off her shoes and setting them down next to her mother's shoes in the neat organized row, she rang on her house's doorbell, which was answered almost immediately by her parents. They questioned her, in Japanese, as to where she had been for so long. She ignored her parents, and asked them back in English, "What's for dinner tonight? And... who's over?"

Her parents reacted immediately to their daughter's question as if they had never met someone less intelligent than her. They began muttering to each other in disappointment, shaking their heads at both her question, and her continued refusal to speak their native language. Obviously, Autumn was expected to remember something they told her at some other point in time, about someone really important coming over for dinner that night. Also quite obviously, she *didn't* remember.

"Mr. Fukushima is over today. We were about to close a deal with him, but he is rather upset at the moment. He does not want to begin eating dinner until he has the soothing music we had promised him. You know you'll be punished later. Just go, play *right now*. The 5th movement of the piece Mr. Chan and I wrote will be suitable, I assume. Go!" her mother said to her, as her father had already walked back to the kitchen to assure their guest that he would soon have what he had been promised.

"Fine. Just give me some time to study later. I need some time to be... alone. Okay?" Autumn responded to her mother, the inflection of her voice dripping with venom. She was tired of her parents parading her in front of whatever important person they had over, just so that they could show off their status, their "beautiful" daughter, and whatever else they could pull out of their ridiculous, finely woven silk sleeves.

Not waiting for her mother to answer her remark, she strutted towards her piano, opening up the bench upon reaching it and pulling out multiple sheets of music, setting them up on the stand of her piano. Also, she set her metronome to start running, tipping from one side to the other – the constant, steady ticking noises were just what she needed, something predictable in her life for once: something that wouldn't disappear on her when she needed it.

The 5th movement of the Kizuno Sonata wasn't a difficult piece; rather, it required a lot of movement on the piano - her fingers constantly darting up and down the keys - to fulfill the requirements of the contrasting sections in the piece. Her mother held great pride in the piece, and hell would be brought down upon Autumn if she couldn't it perfectly – whenever she practiced, it would be that piece she spent the most time on, for obvious reasons.

Stretching her fingers, she began doing a quick warm-up up and down the piano, an arpeggiating F major scale with only her thumbs and pinkies, various chord warm ups moving up and down octaves. The whole time, the metronome ticked away, keeping a steady beat for her, as she internalized it, feeling her heart filling in the offbeat for it. *Tick thump, tick thump.* Then, she stopped, and the silence fell heavily upon everyone in the house: she was about to begin.

Very quietly, the first sounds of the piano were heard and pronounced clearly in the large living room, echoing strongly into the dining room and the other neighbouring rooms. Autumn's fingers were lost in a flurry, each of them taking on a life of its own.

Beautifully weaving notes together, she dove through the piece. One minute in, two minutes in, the scales weren't giving her any trouble at all, and her mother sat back, more at ease seeing the positive results of her daughter's practice as the notes continued floating through the dining room air. A wonderful atmosphere began developing slowly, forming itself around her notes: the centerpiece to their dinner had arrived.

Their meal was eaten, for the most part in silence; everyone listening intently to Autumn, playing on their family's concert hall piano, an import from Japan, a top-quality product – Autumn had always known it wasn't a meaningful present to her though: it was just another object for her family to show off to the guests.

Eventually,, dinner was finished, and Mr. Fukushima applauded happily, as the sonata concluded shortly after, more than a half hour of the light sound of the piano ringing through his ears, everything melodically pleasing. Her parents merely stared at her, nodding ever so slightly in approval of how she played the piece, though she would obviously be reprimanded by her mother later because the performance wasn't perfect. Her performances were never *perfect,* nor was it possible that they ever would be. Perfection was the expectation though, and therefore, she could never do better than what was expected of her, and her parents in turn were also never impressed with her.

Autumn stood up from the piano bench, allowing her parents' guest to pat her on the shoulder. She shook his hand, and turned around, walking up to her room, picking up her bag from the foot of the stairs on the way. Half way up the stairs, she stopped walking, pulled out her sketch book, and opened it. On the page she opened to, she saw a lily, a symbol of purity, of refined beauty: something that should mean nothing to her, as she knew she could never be like that, like the splendid lily on the page before her.

A tear formed, dripped onto the page, and flowed down the petals of the lily, falling into the depths of the pond on which the lily was drawn. The flat surface of the water stayed disturbed only for a second – and it went back to being still, as if it had never been touched by the sorrows of her world.

A symbol of purity.

Autumn shut the notebook as she began to cry, concealed behind the figurative wall she created for herself with her drawings. Even behind her walls, she still felt exposed, as the forest in which she hid began to burn down around her.

Chapter 15

A quick kiss on the lips, a couple of hushed good byes, and another pair of subtle "I love you's", then Cindy was off to get back home before her mother came looking for her.

They both knew she was soon to be scolded for being out after her "curfew" seeing as it was already a full two minutes past 6:00pm.

Oh the troubles of having a traditionally Chinese mother.

Though the notion of her mother waiting for her was rather embarrassing, she was still scared of what her mother might come up with as a punishment, so she hugged Damian one last time and then ran off in the dull grey night. Hoping to reach home soon, before it got dark, and before her mother would get too worried, she was in a hurry, dashing away from Damian's house - even if she only lived a three minute walk from it. You could really never know what might happen if her mother got worried.

Truthfully though, it didn't matter to her how much her mother was worrying. She only really wanted to get home faster to keep working on her composition, to safely tuck herself into her musical sanctuary, to write away while imagining guitar strings being picked along with her piano keys being struck. That was all she had to look forward to when she got home: dinner was only tasteless food she needed to eat to survive, so she never really looked forward to it. Differently shaped tofu each night wasn't really something to look forward to, no matter how she looked at it.

Unlocking the door, she took off her shoes and smelt something new for dinner that night, the aromas wafting lightly outside of the kitchen: not deceived, she suspected, and suspected correctly, that her mother had just added something new to the tofu.

Upon further inspection in the kitchen, she was disappointed, but not surprised, to see a new brand of soy sauce put over all her food – it *did* release a nice smell when it was used to cook, but it really didn't taste all that different.

Still, thanking her mother for putting the dinner on the table by herself, she slowly ate her dinner, not thinking about her chewing and swallowing, not taking any time to savour the food: it was always there, never tasted any different, and always consisted of basically the same thing. That was the thing about her house's atmosphere… though she was starving, and hadn't eaten since her lunch; she didn't really feel like eating dinner in silence, across from her mother, exchanging awkward stares every few seconds.

The last spoonful of food leaving her bowl and entering her mouth, she let the spoon clink lightly as it landed back in her small ceramic bowl. She brought her bowl over to the sink and set it down, running some water over it. She never really needed to wash the dishes, because her mother always seemed to be able to do it better - saving an extra millilitre of water, spending 5 less seconds than Cindy did to complete job - so she just let her mother do the job, and thanked her for it.

"Thanks Mom," Cindy said to her mother, not looking back as she left the kitchen and began walking up the stairs.

Finally, she would be able to do what she had been waiting to do ever since she left Damian's house: work on "Relentless Reminiscence".

Not even bothering to take a shower, she sat right down in her chair. She considered what she would do, as she didn't really want to go to bed that night stinking, and she came up with her solution: she would just wash her hair in the morning... or something. She couldn't leave for a shower even if she wanted to – the notes on the page were pulling her in, and wouldn't let her go: she had to finish the piece before that Friday, and have it done perfectly. It would make up for the four months they had lost... wouldn't it?

All that time that she might never be able to recover - it tore at her. There was something in her mind that kept telling her that her composition would fix it all though, that it would stop the feeling of loss from tearing her down from the inside, that her composition was all that mattered. And that was how it really felt.

Staring into the lines, the spaces, Cindy kept crafting melodies and rhythms, scribbling and notating on the sheet of paper; she became lost within her own creation, while hoping and praying to a God she didn't believe in that everything would work well - that Damian would like what she had done for him.

There was one last thought on her mind though, that she refused to admit was there: she hoped that her piece really would fix the hole those four months apart from Damian had left in her heart.

A quick kiss on the lips, a couple of hushed good byes, and another pair of subtle "I love you's", then Cindy was off to get back home before her mother came looking for her.

Cindy hadn't even looked back as she marched off into the darkness, determinedly headed towards her house: that was the last thing he saw as he shut the front door of his house and walked upstairs, eager to get back to work.

Walking into his room, he quickly thought of how he was going to allocate his time as he picked up his guitar, just to set it back down by his bedside table, looming ominously over his notebook.

Snatching up all his English notes from their scattered position on his bed, re-ordering them and placing them neatly back into his binder, his room was back to how it had been earlier that day: spotless, as he usually kept it.

Glancing over how clean his room was, Damian staggered over to his work desk and sat down in the chair. His lack of sleep was just beginning to get to him.

Still holding his binder, Damian set it down at the foot of his desk, and then sat up straight again. He opened the large drawer directly below the top of his desk slightly, and pulled out his new piece.

He wanted to try to put himself into Cindy's shoes, to try looking at the piece like she would whenever she tried writing something for him... she had always tried to surprise him with compositions of hers in the past, where she would write them completely without hearing what they would sound like even once – and every single one of them ended up sounding beautiful all the same.

His brain apparently didn't feel like complying with him though, and his knowledge in musical theory sank through the ground and was lost, so he walked back over to his bedside table, and reluctantly picked up his guitar. He was tired and didn't feel like reaching over his guitar to write, but he would need it to work – for that night at least.

He got right off to work with his pen poised over his music, ready to set off on his musical voyage and compose up a storm in his tiny little room.

He wrote for what seemed to have been an eternity, and stopped to see how much progress he made.

A subtle glance at the clock on his bedside table told him that it was already 8:05pm, meaning he had sat at his work desk for nearly 2 hours, and he was done little more than three lines of bad quality music. His scales were depressingly out of tune; his chords just weren't harmonized with each other - and then came the fact that he was just too lazy that night to fix any of it. He was a hopeless cause in his own views, and he couldn't deny it.

He was disappointed in himself... it seemed like the musical part of his brain just died after Cindy left to go home. Still determined to write something for her though, he wrote on, thinking of taking a shower soon and going to bed, but that wasn't a satisfying thought in any way.

He needed to finish his piece for Friday - that would show Cindy what he had done over the four months they were apart, and what he did the few hours a day they were apart from each other: he thought of her. Sometimes it felt like she was the only thing on his mind, and that she meant everything to him.

And then, it was a Fresh Beginning, to an end that didn't necessarily happen, for a reason that would always remain unknown to him.

A new page in the composition of his life.

Chapter 16

Tuesday morning rolled around as Damian opened his eyes abruptly, staring at the ceiling, waking up to the sound of his alarm clock. Another night had gone by: he only had four days left to work until their anniversary: his and Cindy's.

He definitely still had some more planning to do, but before then... his arm reached in the vague area of his bedside table by his head as he brought down his hand, silencing the alarm within seconds.

7:00am, the same time as every morning since his dad had given up on exercising in the morning, days after he had begun his obsession with... Damian shuddered... weight loss. The only thing his father seemed to be losing was sleep, really, so he stopped.

Besides the slight cringing at memories of his dad trying to feel younger, it was a serene morning as always. With the sun shining through his paper-thin curtains, every particle of dust in his room was visible. He stepped out of bed just like he did every morning to get ready to go to school. That didn't mean he wanted anything to change in his repetitive schedule though. Normal, repetitive and boring: they were his safe zones.

The short trip over the cold hardwood flooring of his room into the equally cold tiled floor in his bathroom, occasionally stepping in warmer, sun-bathed spots, was also the same as it was every morning.

The mechanical processes that followed: combing his hair, brushing his teeth, and washing his face – they were all part of his routine, the simplicity of his tasks adding to the peacefulness of his morning: they were things he did every day, the exact same way.

The running of cold water in the sink woke him up slightly, bringing him out of his dazed feeling of insensitivity, into the presence of his surroundings. He bared his teeth widely, checking his smile in the mirror quickly; a real smile overtook his bared teeth, genuine satisfaction in what he saw in the mirror. His smile was still as bright as ever, but for once, it was what he wanted to see.

After finishing with his quick morning shower, Damian opened the door to his bathroom, already changed into a fresh pair of dark navy jeans and a light blue t-shirt, and stepped out of the bathroom.

He was about to have the same breakfast he had every morning: his soggy eggs, sunny side up, with trace amounts of salt, eaten with whole wheat bread and a tall glass of orange juice.

One foot on the staircase, he began to wonder how he managed to live so... routinely every single day, and not go insane. He thought about it, and figured he didn't live *completely* routinely though. There was always something guaranteed to stir up some trouble for him, something to push the envelope... to make things more interesting.

And that was about when his house's phones began to ring loudly, blasting through the hallways, putting an abrupt end to his peaceful morning.

7:10am: a full half hour earlier than she would have

woken up a month prior for school. Cindy's alarm rang, and she rolled happily out of bed... and fell onto the floor.

Sitting up and rubbing her elbows, she groaned to herself: miscalculating how large her bed was always ended awkwardly.

Still, she sat up and gazed blankly at her door, until she realized she should probably get up and out of her room to get ready for school. She hoped she'd have some time to talk to Damian before the first bell rang if she managed to get ready earlier. Time management and being organized had suddenly begun to exist again for her – it felt wonderful.

She felt in the mood for a shower, because of feeling filthy in her clothes, after putting it off for several hours the previous night. She quickly grabbed several pieces of clothing, threw them on to the bed she had just tumbled out of, and brought her towel with her in to the bathroom.

Turning on the water, the sound of it running soothed her. She knew she would probably be in the tub for a while, so she set up her alarm again to go off at 7:25am, so she could have some time to prepare her books and eat breakfast: also concepts new to her after 4 months of effectively ignoring them.

The tub was nearly three quarters of the way full by the time she finished brushing her teeth vigorously, and brushing her hair with equal vigour in an attempt to straighten it: her hair was strange, and if it wasn't moderately straight when she went into the tub, it became a horribly fluffy mess when she came out. Cindy couldn't wait to just sink into the hot water of the tub and think.

Thinking in the bath tub: to Cindy, it has always seemed a lot easier to get her thoughts through clearly, to process them in her brain, when she was unclothed and in a basin of hot water. The thought of it wasn't all too perplexing though as the water's effects immediately set in, and she mindlessly scrubbed herself down, her mind set on wondering about what she had done last the previous night.

The night before, for hours after she left Damian's house, she worked on the composition she had written for them, and it had worked rather well.

Again, she didn't have guitar strings to simulate the harmony for her, but she had a vast enough amount of knowledge that she was capable to write out approximately one minute of melody for them with no problem: the minute of melody she wrote would probably also be used repeated in her song, as a sort of chorus.

Her piece was something of a rondo, the chorus played, with differentiating parts played between each occurrence of it. There was to be a beginning and an ending, with traces of the chorus, yet again: the chorus would be when the two instruments treated each other as equals, and sang at the same pitches, same volumes. That was the centerpiece of her song, and she took pride in it. She could feel just as important as he was, whenever she wrote parts for him in her songs.

Though, in terms of her music writing the previous night, once she had finished writing her chorus, she had felt drained, her melodic reservoirs emptied for the night, at which point she put down her piece, but did not set down her pen.

Instead, feeling yet another rush of creativity, this time of a different sort, she delved into the depths of her backpack, and pulled out something she hadn't written in for what seemed like years: her old scrap notebook.

Staring into it, though she lacked any sort of inspiration, she tried writing a poem, her first poem ever outside of academic purposes: Metronome.

> A steady beat,
> Never dying out,
> Always here for me,

As I hear its ticking,
From side to side.

This is the only thing left,
That remains in my life,
Entirely predictable,
The one thing I can still rely on:
A metronome.

But when I need it most,
The soothing mindless throbbing,
The heartbeat to my music,
It halts,
And everything falls out of control.

She remembered that, reading her poem over directly after writing it, she was dissatisfied with herself. Her writing conventions had gotten rusty. They would really need some work later on.

In the meantime, coming back to her current position - sitting in her bath tub, day-dreaming away - she shut off the water and climbed out, then dried herself off.

She would be at school in less than 20 minutes. For the first time in a long time, she was excited to go, and was going to be on time.

Today is a good day, she thought to herself.

"Don't forget. I'll see you right after school today. Outside of your house. Alright?" she said, slightly menacingly, though clearly she was trying to keep the inflection out of her voice.

"Alright... I'll see you then, don't worry about it. I'm really sorry about before though, really I am," he told her, though, really he wasn't. Damian hung up right after his last reply.

He would be dreading the final bell of the day. It would be the sound that foreshadowed his meeting with Autumn, whether he liked it or not. She would become a forest fire, demanding to know everything when she saw him, and he would just be a tree, caught somewhere within her destructive path.

It seemed like it would be a long day.

At Perten Senior High, the first bell rang as Cindy and Damian were walking through the halls together towards their English class.

When they arrived, the teacher wasn't there, and would be late as always, so they stood directly outside the door along with about half the class. Everyone was just standing around, waiting for the teacher to show up, chattering over the buzz of other students passing by, talking to people around them: the usual daily commotions.

"So, this Friday... you want to go to the beach, then the park, drop by George's café, and then go to your house?" Damian listed, repeating after Cindy, as she excitedly planned out how they would spend the landmark of their 4th year dating. *Fourth year together*.

"Yes! Oh my goodness... I can't wait! What did you get me?" she asked playfully, batting her eyelashes at him, smiling lightly.

"You'll just have to wait and see," Damian responded, smiling back at her. "I'm pretty sure you'll like it. Pretty sure: no guarantees though.

Knowing what he was talking about, he knew that he was referring to his composition. Damian still wanted to keep it a secret from Cindy: she really would enjoy the surprise it involved, having him break out into a new song that he wrote just for her, three days from then.

"Well, same goes for my present to you then. Who knows, hm? We'll just have to wait and see what you think of it," her eyes twinkled as she said this, leaving it truly a mystery to him as to what she had planned.

"Alright, so, right after the bell goes on Friday, we go, and we'll be back at your house by... 7 o'clock?" Damian confirmed.

"No, my mom says we can be out until 8. I think we can spend a little more time on the beach... you know, stay to watch the sun set... that kind of thing," Cindy's eyes began to stare off, at some spot about two metres in front of her, imagining the beauty of the scene, standing next to him after four years of being together.

Damian got the picture Cindy was trying to convey to him, but yet again, this image was interrupted by one of Autumn, dancing along in front of his eyes, the silhouette of a stranger, someone he didn't know, yet did, flashed before him.

"Are you absolutely sure you want to come over to my house today? Our kitchen looks terrible right now... can you give me a few minutes to go to my house to clean up?" Damian was thinking fast – what could he do to discreetly ask Cindy to go home, and give him a few minutes to talk to Autumn?

"Well, yeah, of course I want to come over. We can work on Autumn Fantasies, right? We can have more time to do that. I don't mind your kitchen, really. I'll be fine," she insisted even further. Her mind didn't seem to want to be changed: obviously his excuse wasn't enough to keep her out.

Damian stared at her for a few seconds, continuing to stroke her thin, delicate hair, standing in front of their English classroom.

He braced himself for the worst to come later.

"Alright then. We'll walk right back to my house at the end of the day."

Chapter 17

Yet again, the bell to Perten Senior rang as it did every day, announcing the end to another day. *Signalling release.*

Students in all directions suddenly seemed to wake up right at that moment, welcoming the joyful tintinnabulation of the bells, picking up their books and running out of their classrooms, a short "see you tomorrow miss" or "see you tomorrow sir" for their teachers on the way out.

Cindy and Damian ended up being two of the last people to leave the classroom as they had been too pre-occupied writing back and forth on a piece of paper during class to begin packing for the end of the day. Five minutes before the bell went, when everyone else had already begun picking up their notebooks and stuffing them into their backpacks, Cindy and Damian were still huddled over their paper, having a written conversation.

As the bell had just rung, the hallways would be packed, and they would be for the next 10 minutes or so. For that reason, the couple packed up their things slowly, but did not get up.

Sitting down in their seats, chairs that hadn't moved for the last hour, they continued to talk about what they had been talking about before class started, and during class on paper. Except then, out loud again, the pens and paper put away deep in their bags.

"Wait, wait... so you want to go *where* this Friday?" Damian asked Cindy, clarifying for what seemed like the 10th time as to where she wanted to go on their 4th year anniversary, as she kept changing her mind. Every few minutes, she added more and more items to the list, also deciding she didn't want to go to several of the places she originally wanted to.

So confusing, Damian thought to himself.

"Alright. First, we're going to go down to the plaza, because I want to pick something up, and we can drop in on George's. Then, we're going down to the park that's across from the plaza, to go to our bench, and then we're going to make it to the beach for the sunset. After that, we'll go back to my house, but we'll rent a movie on the way, so we have something to do. You can stay at my house until 11... so."

She just stopped talking, her voice suddenly cutting off, taking a deep breath after her rant about where she wanted to go: she was smiling at him. And he smiled back.

"Cool. I'll just tell my dad that I'll be out late then. I can't wait..." Damian told her, genuinely excited, but he thought back to earlier that day. "Are you sure you don't want to go back to your house to prepare or anything before you come to my house?..."

"I'm sure I'll be fine. Are you trying to say that I don't look good right now? Hm?" she inquired, and though she was joking, he gave up. She was going to his house, and she wasn't going to like what she saw waiting for them in front of it.

He sighed under his breath.

They began walking to his house together, holding hands and, step after step in silence, trying to figure out what the other person was thinking about.

Across the street from the neighbour's opposite him in their well-kept house, Autumn sat in front of Damian's house, on a green transformer. The vague humming of the electricity deep within the large metal box was nearly hypnotic: she was staring off into the sky, constantly checking back at her watch: it read 2:40pm.

He was going to arrive soon.

On cue, Damian walked around the corner, but her jaw dropped as she saw he held another girl's hand. That girl... Autumn hadn't seen her before: *where had she been for the months she lived here?*

The apparent couple approaching her quickly, she sat, still as a stone, staring at them, waiting for him to come close enough that she could talk to him at a normal volume, not wanting to shout awkwardly at him.

The girl looked upset with him, judging by her posture. She was gripping his hand tighter than would be normal, looking to be asking him questions and frantically trying to figure out who the girl sitting on the transformer was.

The thought amused her.

So far, she had given up on her feeble attempts at drawing love: she could not feel it, and from what she knew, she would never feel it. Never.

"Hi, Damian," she said to them, feeling in power, again. It felt good. She didn't have to be the one on her knees, helpless to what other people were doing to her. She stood up then, trying to make eye contact with him.

Frowning, Damian finally looked back at Autumn, staring blankly straight into her eyes but still not answering her greeting. Furrowing his eyebrows and biting his lip, his expression was unfathomable for a moment. His eyes remained expressionless, his stress not reaching them, and in that moment, he seemed frustrated, but with who, it wasn't clear.

In fact, it almost pained Autumn as she looked at him and the girl by his side. Well, it *did* pain her, just seeing the girl with him, but she nearly felt bad for confronting him, the last person who broke her heart. *She couldn't let that show though.*

"You know why I'm here. Explain. Now," Autumn said to Damian, several shades too blunt and aggressive – but why *was* she there? He didn't belong to her, hadn't actually promised anything. That might have been true, the fact that she had no right to him, but she wanted him so, so bad. She was only here to chase him. So she *was* on her knees.

He was still silent though, standing stiffly there, looking as if he couldn't decide what to do; whether he would run away from the scene and escape the confrontation or respond to her was unapparent.

Autumn watched him, trying to receive some hint of what he was going to do, whether or not she would get to talk to him, when her thoughts were interrupted.

"Who are you? And… why *are* you here?" Cindy demanded of Autumn, glaring intensely at her, not even bothering at the moment to harass Damian on the topic. "What do you want from us?"

Autumn was taken off-guard: she wasn't expecting retaliation from the girl who stood by Damian. She had expected to be able to have some time to talk to Damian, to sort out the whole mess… to just be alone with him once again – she wanted so badly to relive the happy memories she had of him, that one happy hour of her life. She wanted to, but she couldn't.

"There's nothing I want from *you*. I just want to talk to Damian about something, that's all," Autumn retorted, still attempting to keep up her aggressive image, not allowing any weakness to show in the conversation, especially not to the girl.

Autumn thought to herself spitefully, *That lucky* -

"Why do you want to talk to him though? What's this all about? Damian… what's she talking about? Who *is* this girl?" Cindy asked, finally turning to face him, but easing her glare to a concerned stare at him. She didn't know what to do.

"Look, my name's Autumn, I just happen to know Damian and need to talk to him about something right now,"

Autumn said, also easing her tone and gaze, calming down to prepare for a sort of false compromise with the girl.

"Well, my name's Cindy and I still demand to know exactly what you want to talk to my boyfriend about."

And Autumn choked on the words she was about to toss back at Cindy.

So that's who this girl is... it had all just began to make sense to Autumn: yet again, she was the one under the artist's paintbrush, with no control over her life. And, also yet again, she was posing for the artist; whoever it was, they had their brush poised over her life's story, and prepared to paint her yet another tragedy.

Panic-stricken as he held Cindy's hand, they walked around the corner towards his house, and he noticed something several houses before she did: the person who was sitting on the transformer in front of his house.

Calmly sitting there, as if they had all the time in the world, waiting for someone, he knew who it was. And Cindy would too, soon enough. He just hoped to goodness that Autumn wouldn't announce her name, as that would be just enough to expose his "Autumn Fantasies".

He scoured his mind in search of something he could use at the last minute to get Cindy over to her house, to excuse himself from talking to Autumn, to get into his house without running into Autumn. All of these ideas: they were drowned out in the screaming inside of his head. *What was he going to do?*

"Who is that? Did some new family move into your area?... How come I've never seen that girl before?" Cindy asked curiously, a dash of worry making its way into her voice. Cindy wanted to know who the girl was.

Damian merely looked back at Cindy, not saying a word. Everything would explain itself soon enough, because there was nothing he could do to get away from talking to Autumn.

Step after step, he felt like he was walking alongside heaven, to go to hell, one foot in front of the other, paving the road for him.

Cindy didn't further question it as the two continued walking. Finally, they reached the boundary of his lawn and the neighbour's lawn: that was when the first word was spoken between the two parties.

"Hi, Damian," Autumn said to him, but it also seemed like it was meant as a threat to Cindy. What had he done to Autumn though? If he had made plans, then cancelled, where was the harm in that? If he didn't want to talk to her, why did she have to chase him down? Why did there have to be retribution for his tiny acts of immorality?

Thinking of a response and still wondering what he could say to explain the whole mess to Cindy, he looked at Autumn, and completely lost control of his mind. He couldn't see a few metres in front of him, as the world became a blur, and he felt himself rooted to the spot, unable to leave the confrontation.

He saw the silhouette of Autumn, and watched it fade out in front of him as he felt himself lose control of his body. The ground melted away from underneath him, the sky decided to become black, and the sun had found its true love and run away.

Everything around him vanished, and soon, he was nowhere. But where was nowhere?

The world, suddenly void of all existence but himself, was no longer so trivial, and he found himself capable of thinking straight, only quiet voices whispering vaguely in the back of his mind were present. This sanctuary from the world and all of its dishonesty made him feel both lost and found in the first minute he had stumbled upon it.

Mulling over his thoughts in the surreal zone he found himself standing in, he considered all of the events that had taken place in the past week: first he had found a girl who he thought he liked, decided differently, asked out his ex-girlfriend again, gotten back together with her, and was now in an awkward confrontation with both of them.

Really, it didn't seem so complicated laid out before him like that, and he felt satisfied being able to figure out to some extent what was going on. But what *was* he going to do?

Then, suddenly, something materialized before him, slowly taking form as he tried to figure out what it was: within seconds, before him stood a giant, full-length mirror. Truly confused, he looked into it, and saw himself. Just himself. There had to be some sort of relevance behind the mirror though.

Watching himself in the mirror, scratching his head, both inside and out side of the mirror, crossing his arms, deep in thought, and lost in some figurative world, all he saw was himself.

Analyzing his every aspect carefully as he looked at himself, he found the problem as he thought it over again… that was all it was. All he saw was himself.

Still rooted to the spot, he tried to lean towards the mirror, to get a closer look at it, attempting to find some sort of clue it. As he got closer though, it ascended high above him, the dark world lighting up again, returning him to reality.

"Oh… I'm sorry. I… I didn't realize. I'll leave you two alone then… Damian. Why? I don't care right now, because I know I don't matter to you. I never did… but why?" Autumn had begun to cry, looking down at the ground, and she turned and walked away. *Why?*

"I… I don't know," Damian muttered, still dazed from his figurative journey, wondering how he was still conscious.

She was too far away to hear him though, keeping a steady pace in her stride away from him. Damian turned to Cindy and frowned apologetically at her, repeating himself.

"I really don't know."

Chapter 18

They sat next to each other silently in his room; the lack of any noise in the air around them generated a sort of tension. The four months of time they had spent apart was back, visiting them, a subtle reminder to what had happened before.

No explanation to the events that had occurred earlier that day was offered to her.

Cindy was lying down on his bed, facing the ceiling, holding the script for King Lear in front of her at about reading distance, diving through the text in Act 2. She didn't feel in the mood for music, and so she was doing English: Damian noticed her behaviour, and knew he was expected to do something. Soon.

He would break the tension in the air soon, but, in that moment, he was too occupied scribbling down notations on his sheet music. Knowing Cindy wasn't planning on talking any time soon, or making the first move towards him, he was openly working on his new composition, the two sheets of its content side by side on his desk. Staring at the page, he knew what he wanted to do, but he just didn't know how to write it down, how to express it so that he would remember how to play it in the future.

Frustrated, he gripped his pencil even tighter, though he knew it wouldn't accomplish anything, and continued to make random notations, re-arranging notes, bumping the pitch upwards slightly on a certain note, changing the chord quality; but nothing was working.

The arpeggios in his song *did* sound lovely as a countermelody to what he was going to sing, but he still couldn't express himself. He had never felt he was able to express himself fully, not out loud, on paper, or in song. And he wanted to, so badly.

No matter what he did, he couldn't figure the song out: apparently, he wasn't in the mood for music either. Realizing this, he set aside his progress and the multitudes of blank pages of sheet music, and took out a piece of lined paper.

Perhaps that was how he was to express himself. So he wrote, placing the title on the page last, though it would clearly be read first by anyone looking through his work: Recognize.

> Gently greeting him,
> Shaking his hand,
> A friendly exchange,
> As he introduces himself.
>
> Smiling innocently,
> He speaks his name,
> Quietly whispering in my ear,
> Hoping not to frighten me.
>
> Upon hearing his name,
> A name I once was not familiar with him,
> I shy away from him,
> Trying not to meet his eye.
> I now know the name of
> *Corruption.*

He frowned at his creation. It was a feeble attempt at expression, but he decided he would have to stick to it either way: there was nothing better he could do right then, if he wasn't able to write his music: to continue working on his music when there were so many loose ends in his life.

Standing up and shoving in his chair, he walked over to the bed and sat near the foot of his mattress, leaving him somewhere near Cindy's feet. Granted that, she wasn't quite as tall as him, standing at about 160cm when he stood at an even 173cm, but he wasn't taller by a whole lot either. The difference in height definitely showed when they were standing though.

Damian looked over at Cindy scrutinizing the text, her lips pursed lightly, adorable really, lying down in his bed like that, her left leg straight out, and her right foot put up towards her body, her knee off the bed.

He inhaled and then exhaled deeply, breaking the silence wordlessly before he began to speak.

"Look… that girl? She just followed me when she saw me the other day. *We* were still… apart, and she saw me alone, outside of my house, with my guitar. Don't ask… I just needed to, you know, let things go, and since then, she wouldn't leave me alone," Damian stuck to something near the truth, placing a lot more fault on Autumn than himself, really having no concern for her. He didn't want to take the blame. And it hit him hard, as he realized he was only seeing himself in the mirror that was set before him. He wasn't seeing Autumn in his mirror, even when she didn't even have one to look into.

All she had was a window, and all she saw through it was him.

Cindy continued to stare at the book, but her eyes slowed down crossing the page, finishing up a sentence, or perhaps a passage. She heard what he had said, acknowledged it with a small nod, but she still hadn't responded verbally – he already felt a tiny bit better though, as it didn't feel like he was lying to her, and it didn't seem like she was too upset with the fact that they had been confronted.

"Do you want any help? Or, do you want to start working on that piece again?"

"Heck yes! Oh my goodness, I couldn't wait for you to ask," Cindy replied, looking slightly happy again, setting down the Shakespearian text and sitting up, grabbing Damian's hands and looking at him, she smiled lightly, perhaps hiding some sort of feelings she had inside, but responded like she would if she were happy.

"Let's."

Autumn had been home for about an hour, the time standing at about 5:00pm according to the large grandfather clock above her stairwell that chimed monotonously through the night at every hour, the sound of it breaking through the calm silence Autumn had enveloped herself in.

The hallway remained silent, not bothering to take into account that there was a person in its vicinity, and it sullenly watched Autumn as she stood motionlessly in the middle of the threshold.

Realizing she should probably move - out of the main hallway at least - she grabbed a sheet of tissue paper from the kitchen before she walked slowly up the wooden staircase to go to her room, and lie down on her bed.

The tissue absorbed her tears, at least temporarily hiding whatever pain that showed on her face as she lay down on her firm, queen-size mattress. She lay on top of the bed sheets and blanket knit for her by her loving grandmother, who had passed away for over two years.

Every time Autumn found herself lying in bed, whether it was after getting home from a stressful day at school, or about to go to sleep late in the night, she felt like the blanket was embracing her, acting as her grandmother until she could meet her grandmother once again.

Thinking of the gravestone, she remembered how it had been cold and lifeless when she had visited it two weeks ago, even in the radiating sun light. She could still see the text engraved on it, flashing before her eyes: *Hoshi Kizuno, mother of 4 children, two boys, two girls. Grandmother to 9, and more to come; she will be forever remembered, as here she lies, watching us from above, and from within.*

It never felt like her family remembered her grandmother though, as they gave away all of her possessions, trying to rid the house of any memories of the old lady, Autumn's mother's mother.

Autumn fought against it though, trying to keep as many bits of her grandmother alive in the house as possible, and succeeding only a tiny bit: her parents couldn't get rid of *everything*.

Autumn still felt her grandmother watching her, even as her parents continued to try to make her disappear. She could still see the caring, hazy brown eyes staring at her, not fully seeing her without the glasses on the edge of her nose, but still watching over her all the same. With her grandmother gone, who still really cared about her? *Who would be there for her?...*

The tears ran down Autumn's face as she thought about it, holding the blanket close to her, wishing her grandma could still be with her. Embracing it almost felt like it could bridge the unsurpassable gap between her and her grandma. Autumn's grandma was like a mother to her, a proper one, and like a friend, a best friend. She felt the tears continue flowing; landing all around her, the blanket, her memories... her sketch book lay open on the floor in front of her. And she made a decision.

If she couldn't draw love, she would draw pain.

Chapter 19

The faint beeping of Damian's alarm woke him up, as he straightened his back in his chair, rubbing his eyes groggily. After Cindy had left his house the previous night, he had fallen asleep at his desk, face planted firmly on the wooden desk top after working nearly all night on his composition. The progress he saw before his eyes, even at 7:30am in the morning, was impressive.

A bright Wednesday morning, he was unwilling to turn around for fear that the light from the sun would blind him temporarily, leading to some stumbling around. Awkward behaviour in the morning wasn't something he enjoyed doing. *Tripping over his feet*, he thought to himself, *catching his fall against the bathroom door. Point proven.*

His poem from the previous night... thinking back to Autumn's expression as she ran from him... he felt guilty of something serious. It felt like what it might have been like to have openly slapped her in public... he felt like he had caused her so much pain, and that there was no way to fix that. He only saw himself and what he wanted – nowhere in his mind did Autumn's feelings hold any relevance, and he was truthfully sorry to her for that.

Sighing, he pushed his chair back and stood up, stretching his spine, reaching his arms high up in the air, seemingly reaching up, asking for help from some sort of higher power; except he was an atheist, following in the path of his father.

There had to be a reason the world wasn't perfect, and so, the disorder in daily life, over long periods of time, in small areas, large areas... there couldn't possibly be anything on or off the Earth with that much power over humans. Feeling helpless, it gave him no one to blame his troubles on but himself. Either way, he had never felt very strongly about religion.

Damian closed his eyes, thinking back to the previous night again: Cindy's unquestioning acceptance of his apology and explanation to what had happened ... her faith in him that made it so that he didn't have to explain his sudden silence yesterday: he had found love, and he knew it.

Maybe that was why he wasn't ever completely satisfied with his musical works. They were his art form, his outlet for his emotions, and for once in a long time, he was feeling something without limits, that he couldn't put down on paper: love.

Without being able to write it down, to express himself with notes and rhythms, he couldn't show anyone else what this love felt like. And so, again, he felt utterly alone.

When she opened her eyes, the sky was still dark, and she was still lost within the night when other people in Perten had found their way to sunlight.

Autumn closed her eyes again, and pushed the blanket off of herself. Feeling the warm sunlight come in her open window, shining onto her face, she began to rub her eyes gently, feeling how sore they were after spending hours crying the previous night. *Crying herself to sleep.* Whether she was crying for her grandmother, or herself though, she couldn't remember.

Sitting upright abruptly, as she would be expected to be ready to go to school in about 20 minutes by her parents, the clock in the kitchen downstairs had just chimed six times, loudly telling anyone who cared to listen that it was 6 in the morning.

What a sad life the clock had to live, really... when no one cared to really listen to it for any amount of time more than a second, only enough to hear the first chime, to know that it was the next hour. Everyone always knew about what hour it was, so they didn't listen any longer than they needed to, leaving the clock chatting with itself, announcing loudly into the open air what time it was.

Autumn quickly stretched out each of her arms and her legs, and then stood up, shaking her hair up a tiny bit on the way to the bathroom, trying to get an idea of how curly it had become in her sleep. In the middle of her dazed state, she had washed her hair the previous night, as she did every night, so that she could manage to get ready on time in the morning to get to school.

Her days started the same way all the time, and ended about the same way each night. She started her days dully, thinking back to what the last night had been like, not remembering any details, but knowing exactly what she had done, crying herself to sleep – and her nights ended her days with bitter tears that she couldn't find reason behind, as she couldn't remember why she had shed them during or after the daily ritual.

She thought of herself as hopeless, like a sheet of paper in the wind: she knew she was smart, was able to do things, but the moment even the lightest wind blew by, she could no longer hold her ground – she was blown along with the dust in the wind, no more important than each tiny particle, following along only until the wind dissipated, leaving her stranded, lost, unfamiliar with where she had been left.

Each and every time.

Up before the sunrise, Cindy shined like the glass prism she kept on her bedside table as a novelty, projecting her own rainbow upon her own figurative wall, with her own source of sunlight: Damian.

After she had gotten back from his house the previous night, this time without peeking at any of his poetry, she had felt inspired, prepared to write a piece of her own; just to see where it would go.

She decided this time to stick by something she knew well: what it felt like to have to leave Damian each night. So, she wrote "Exigent", five minutes before slipping into bed at 11:54pm.

> Spreading my wings,
> Gently floating in the wind,
> Landing on this beautiful flower,
> And stopping to rest,
> Finding sanctuary at last.
>
> The petals embrace me,
> And I return the touch,
> Gently exchanging silent words,
> Sentences neither of us can speak,
> The wind gently blowing by us.
>
> Suddenly, the urgency grows,
> As the wind follows in pace,
> The time runs low,
> And the moment has come,
> When we must say our farewells,
> *Hopefully to meet once again.*

Recalling the poem that she wrote, the only thing on her mind being Damian and breathing, her heart skipped a few beats. What was she going to do if they were separated again?

She sighed, slightly exasperated with herself. It was barely 5:00am and she was awake, feeling energetic, and missing her boyfriend already.

Skipping across her room, she snatched papers she had left all over her shelf, and ordered them, straightening them out with a short, firm tap on the desk.

These pieces of paper, scrap concepts to be used in her song, a short line of melody that she liked here, progressing chords that she wanted to use there, a guitar and piano part, harmonized beautifully in her mind, quickly jotted down on paper... everything imaginable that could be added in to her song, she had plotted out at random intervals throughout school, at home, and even in the few minutes after dinner she felt incapable of doing anything but sit.

Slowly, she filed through her various little jot notes, things she was afraid she would forget over the time between when she thought them up, and when she would be able to get to her room. Relentless Reminiscence, hiding deep within the drawer of her desk, was always waiting to be edited further whenever she had the time. Whatever she felt she could use, she quickly inserted, comparing the new melody to the old one. As always, she would try to see if they would conflict if she used them together: she never wanted to waste even one tiny amount of content.

The song - with an apparent pattern for the first half: ascending and descending scales - was a peaceful dance between the two instruments, two lovers singing to each other, happily dancing a swirling dance with each other in a meadow, a pasture perhaps.

When the melody shifted to the second half, with an ingenious chord progression she had thought up, the mood switched: the two instruments were suddenly upset with each other. The piano no longer waited patiently for the guitar to finish its line, and instead began to take over the melody, interrupting the guitar, causing the musical argument to flow smoothly and roughly, alternating at regular intervals, all throughout the piece.

The overlapping notes: it was a violent, heated embrace between the notes of one instrument and the other. The conflict between the instruments was an addition she had only thought of recently, minor changes here and there that she had added, to disturb the tone of her song slightly. She wanted variety in her piece, so that was what she added.

Cindy sighed lightly to herself, and clasped her hands together, resting them on top of her piece, not knowing what to add next: how was she going to resolve the clandestine argument between the guitar and the piano? Where was the solution, the answer that would relieve the tension that had been built up so consistently by the two instruments?

Chapter 20

The paper had been covered in deep, dark smudges, shading applied here and there with small openings, in case something new came up that she wanted to put into them. Otherwise, Autumn's drawing of love had turned into a drawing of pain, and she was loving it.

To her, the piece was beautiful, in its terrible simplicity, and how it was just a large black mass, with its own shape, its own ideas, not willing to conform to anyone or anything, even if it would be so much better off it did. Giving up was always easier, but as she saw herself in the cloud of smoke, she knew neither of them *would*.

An addition to the piece, added in the small hours of the previous night, she had drawn in a glass wall, a slight shining clearness fogged up by the black mass, but still surrounding it, oppressing it, the only obstacle to the otherwise formless and inexorable shape.

An interesting point she decided to add to the glass wall was that at the location where she had drawn a small heart - her own, broken in two pieces, a clear split down the centre - the wall had broken too, a small crack, an opening. Through this opening, her heart, out poured the black mass, and on the piece of paper, it was visible to her, shown in its entirety, tenderly cracked down the middle, exposed to her as a clever visual analogy for the pain she was releasing onto the paper.

Her medium was still a pen, as it had always been. As she continued sketching slowly, she still felt very strongly about her use of visualized literary devices, her black smoke escaping alluding to what might be underneath it all, after the glass wall was smouldered away by the intense heat within, the small images spread throughout the mass of blackened air, polluting the mass further with small symbols for other causes of her pain.

Manipulating her pain into a type of art, she continued forming contour lines up and down the mass, though she was really paying a lot more attention to thinking back to each source of her pain captured in the her picture, soon to be released, out the hole in her heart... or so she hoped would happen once she finished her drawing.

Finger nails pressed into the flesh and skin of her palm, it didn't seem like her rescue was going to come any time soon.

After a few more minutes of drawing, the time barely 6:30am by her guess, Autumn became busy observing her picture, finally taking the time to stop and study it. Her hand had stopped moving, the pen strokes suddenly interrupted by a moment of examination of her piece: and she was actually slightly satisfied looking at what she had drawn over the last day.

Tracing her drawing from the very first stroke on the page, near the bottom-left corner, she looked at the very beginning of all of her pain... it was a very, very small drawing of a map of Perten. The shorelines clearly visible around it, the bordering cities were cut out of the picture; the township of Perten was apparent, openly uninteresting and entirely lacklustre on the page. It lacked any detail, or care, other than to make sure she didn't catch any surrounding cities in the crosshairs, and that she had drawn in every single part of Perten with the dull style she chose. Looking at it, she decided she had captured it perfectly.

Continuing up the line, her finger led her around the rounded edges of the smoke, around the rolling textures of the mass, across the greyscale shimmer shining faintly out of the blackness.

Eventually, she fell upon her next picture: a grand piano. It was the piano in a concert hall back at Tokyo, coincidentally the same model that was here in Perten, in the concert hall behind Perten Senior High. A Yamaha CF series: the crisp and clear ringing tones from the strings being struck within it haunted her.

It wasn't necessarily that particular piano that had caused her any sort of pain though. She admitted it *did* bring back some harsh memories of the hours she had practiced and performed for many people back in Tokyo, but the true source of her pain within the symbol wasn't any particular piano, but just the instrument that she had been forced to learn. Soon, she would make plans to go to the Perten Concert Hall and practice, but in the meantime, she continued to scrutinize her picture.

She realized that, although it had always been what she could do best, even better than her visual art, her little sketches, the occasional painting, her musical skill was the most valued by her parents, and it was the skill that hurt her the most.

Every time she began to play, she ended up feeling like it had drained away her life, wasting away all her time - but she still held her music close to her heart. And so, there it was, her heart, and the hole in it, neighbouring the grand piano.

Near her heart, she had a little circle that had a few scribbles in it, terminations of her feeble attempts of visually rendering what she wanted to draw, but was empty of all but one word. That word was still important to her, even as it caused her pain to look down upon it. In the midst of all her attempts at drawing her source of pain the source of her failure in that moment - rendered to be visually appealing to whatever audience she might have - there was the single word: Damian.

Chapter 21

The tonal colours in Cindy's finger strokes on the keys of the piano rang clearly throughout; the striking resonance of her brilliant music broke through the anticipated silence created by the violins who were some of her friends she saw around the time of her private lessons with the city's best music teacher. The reverberation of her chords rang steadily, harmonized perfectly with the violins, her hectic scales running up and down the keys were astounding and in perfect balance with the violas.

A piece written by their teacher, still untitled, was made for 6 violins, 6 violas and a piano soloist. Completely written by his hand, still not conveyed electronically to his computer as a backup, as electronic sheet music, he had rushed to school that morning to make sure he would make it in time for his first period 12th grade class's rehearsal for their performance on that Friday. Two minutes after the bell, the time standing at 8:32am, Mr. Grey had run into the doors of the concert hall, out of breath, and had handed each and every one of the 13 instrumentalists their parts, saying nothing to each of them but "look it over quickly, we'll be starting with it."

Now only about half of the way through the piece, each and every one of the instrumentalists had begun sweating with fear of messing up, knowing that if their sight-reading wasn't up to shape that Mr. Grey would give them all hell. The anticipation of the inferno that might flare out of the balding old British man scared them into putting in extra effort to stay on time, not to ruin his masterpiece.

Still sitting high on her seat, Cindy was still not the slightest bit worried, playing chord after chord, taking over the melody from the string instruments, handing it back to them when her turn was up. Then, suddenly, in the 2nd movement of the piece, Cindy saw out of the corner of her eye something on the 12th page that threw her off, nearly causing her to be the first one to mess up: it was a CMaj9 chord, arranged exactly like it had been in her own song, Relentless Reminiscence. The chord had even been inverted the same amount of times, put on the exact same pitch as she had placed it.

Composing herself quickly, she played down the 11th page, briskly and efficiently vocalizing each and every note that had been written down by Mr. Grey, realizing that in that moment, he was entirely focussed on her. It wasn't exactly about her though: he was admiring his melody, staring at her, watching her finger movements, analyzing them and making sure they were all precisely how he wanted them.

Within 20 seconds, Cindy had reached the end of the page, and Mr. Grey turned it for her, now standing right over her shoulder, making it apparent that the melodies over the next few pages were his favourite out of the entire song.

"Strings! Pipe down! We have a soloist emerging in this part, an entirely new voice to this song. In fact, I've tried to make it sound like a completely different person playing here, changing up the style. I want to hear it! I said be quieter!" Mr. Grey yelled over the steady tones from the string instruments, confirming Cindy's fears of how important she was to be considered at that point in the song.

Soon, as she reached the top of the page, realization had sunk in that, not only was the first chord the same as what she had written, a quick scan-through of the next few pages while she held the chord verified that the chord progression was more or less the same as she had plotted in Relentless Reminiscence, note for note. The melody Mr. Grey had written was slightly off though: it didn't seem like he had put as much time into it as he could... but who was she to judge her teacher's works?

Suddenly, the stringed instruments were all looking at her, falling silent, though Cindy assumed that they were merely resting because the song had indicated for them to. As the soloist, she was supposed to be the most important part of the song, and she accepted it.

Barely paying attention to the melody at that point, she felt even more comfortable than she had felt before, feeling like she was playing the piece perfectly, all nervousness of having Mr. Grey stare her down from behind had vanished.

The grand piano and Cindy had become one as she imperviously ran through the music, her eyes closed, suddenly unaware of all her surroundings, and acutely sensitive to what she was playing. The melody made interesting turns, jumping all across the keys, sometimes with both her hands in synchronicity, sometimes arguing with each other, overlapping on some keys - but the disagreements only added texture to the piece in her opinion.

Approaching the last bar, her eyes still closed, she finished off with her favourite chord, the CMaj9 she had placed at the beginning of her song – but as she opened her eyes, she realized in horror that Mr. Grey's piece did *not* end with that chord. In fact, the majority of his song had entirely vanished beneath the piece that she had actually been playing without realizing.

The piece the group had played that had had its melody carefully written out entirely by the hand of their teacher, Mr. Grey, was over run by Cindy, and her Relentless Reminiscence.

In silent horror, she stopped playing, bringing her hands off of the piano, the expression on her face changing from a serene indifference to terror, as she slowly turned around to face the man who had written the piece she just ruined. Turning in her seat to face him, the 12 other instrumentalists began to applaud her, and Mr. Grey smiled happily at her, patting her on the shoulder.

"That was beautiful... a lot better than what I'd written down, really. Though I'm under the impression that you didn't pay too much attention to it..." he said to her, not looking one bit upset with her for not playing what was on the paper.

"Before you have a heart attack, afraid that I'll kick your face in for *ruining* my piece, I want you to turn around and actually take one good look at what you would've played if you had played what I wrote down."

Cindy turned in her seat again, this time to look back at her piano - the keys covered in slight amounts of perspiration - and the stand with the music still laid out before her: on pages 12 to 14, after the first 5 chords, there was no more music.

The only things on the pages were blank lines, void of notes, and what she had previously identified as more chord symbols and notes were just scratches in the paper.

Just scratches in the paper.

Wandering around the city of Perten, Autumn had her entire day off after the principal of Forest Peninsula Senior High declared that the day was to be a professional organization day for the school, entirely mandated as they were behind in work in terms of exams coming up in the next week.

That day, she had left her sketch pad at home, and though her bag wasn't any lighter than usual, she felt like it was nearly empty with it slung over her back as she rounded a street corner, heading towards the Perten Concert Hall and hoping it would be empty.

By her clock, school had barely just started, and she was pretty sure the place would be empty, so she might be able to put in an hour or two of practice on the piano, maybe strike up some aural memories of Tokyo she held deep in her mind, hidden away.

Rounding the last corner before she could see the large high school, and the even larger concert hall rising high and wide behind it, she tripped on a crack in the sidewalk, only barely stopping her fall with her hands as she hit the ground.

Autumn turned around even while she lay on the ground, and scowled at the small loose piece of concrete that had caused her wrist to be sprained and the newly-made scrape on her knee to begin burning painfully with exposure to the open air around her. Not wanting anyone to catch her in such a position, openly stretched out on the ground, clutching herself in various areas, whimpering slightly in pain, she stood up and brushed some of the dirt clinging on to her off, back down to the ground.

Back on her feet within seconds of convincing herself the fall wasn't that bad, she began gazing longingly at the concert hall, anticipating seeing the piano inside it. She debated still going though, even if she wouldn't be able to play anything too elaborate with her wrists in their condition, injured by a fall to the ground.

After only about 10 seconds of deliberation, Autumn continued walking towards the concert hall, considerably more carefully, gingerly stepping over anything that could have been a bump in the sidewalk – another cause for falling.

About 10 metres away from the concert hall, she began to hear the faint sound of music being emitted from within the large, black, contoured building. Quite a beautiful song, a very quick one, it sounded like it was being played by the musicians for the first time, with each and every one of them sight-reading at about the same level of confidence: but it still sounded reasonably good.

Clearly, this piece had been written by a concert master: someone with vast knowledge in music, who wrote the piece and practiced writing pieces specifically for that consort of instruments.

Continuing to approach the concert hall, the sounds became more apparent. The harsh ringing of several bows on strings was the loudest in that moment, frantically darting up and down scales, minor, major, in several different modes. There were maybe about five violins and eight violas, though she assumed her guess was probably off by a good amount.

A large rush of chromaticism came by, the composer using several notes outside of the dominant key, probably in allusion to a key change about to occur, and then it happened, all at once.

As Autumn closed the final few steps between her and the building, she walked into the concert hall, seating herself in a chair almost at the very back, about 10 seats away from another person sitting in the dark, watching the group practice. She heard the sound that had haunted her all the way from back in Tokyo.

Upon the striking of the first chord in the solo passage, a major 9th, each and every one of the six violas and six violins (she *was* incorrect, but close at least) fell silent as the soloist on the grand piano – no, *her* grand piano – took over the melody, releasing the tension created by the stringed instruments, cutting smoothly through the scales much more comfortably than was warranted for someone sight-reading the music. The circumstances brought up an inquiry in Autumn's mind: who was the soloist, and who had written this part for him or her? How were they playing it so well?

It sounded nothing like the style the composer of the first part had kept consistent, and it had fixed many errors in harmony that the first composer had in his piece (assuming the old Caucasian man standing beside the piano was the composer). The piece was wonderfully constructed with a certain liveliness, a sort of youthful jump to it that the man would never have achieved... and it was being played with near perfection and a great amount of skill by whoever the soloist was. And who *was* the soloist: this person so beautifully playing the instrument that caused her so much pain in her past?

Autumn knew where the piece was heading, feeling each chord progression as it passed by her, musically appealing in every sense. She had a feeling that whoever had written it was the one playing it in the ensemble. The soloist was someone she knew she admired in that moment, the kind of person who could write an amazing piece and perform it effortlessly, in complete comfort before a group of people.

Then, as the song slowed down slightly, softening then loudening, the final three chords were then played firmly and self-assuredly by the soloist. A perfect cadence finished off the piece, and the ringing of the piano keys stopped after a few seconds, but remained in Autumn's mind for a time afterwards, reminding her of her lessons back in Tokyo.

Her recollection was halted momentarily by the loud applause of the man, and each of the other 12 instrumentalists, six male, six female, three of each gender on each instrument.

It seemed like this was a rehearsal for some sort of a performance, and that was a new piece that was to be played at that performance, whenever and wherever it was to take place.

As everyone continued to applaud, and the teacher said something very quietly to the soloist, the soloist stood up and emerged from behind the grand piano's broad lid, walking over, apparently to thank the other instruments for playing the piece so well with her.

One glimpse of the soloist's face and Autumn shuddered in her seat: it was her.

The lucky charlatan who managed to take Damian from her; there she stood, smiling at all her friends: it was Cindy Lau.

~~~

"That was amazing, Cindy!" Bill yelled, setting down his viola and shaking her hand. "Did you just improvise that, like you usually do?... You know, to piss him off?"

"That's just it... erm... there's this song that I'm writing, and I just kind of played it subconsciously. I swear Mr. Grey was going to kill me right after I finished playing that."

"Oh, I know how you feel, Ms. Lau. But on the contrary, I rather enjoyed that. Would you like to write the part into the piece? You can perform it this Friday if you want," Mr. Grey offered her. He was holding out a black pen, 0.3B, ridiculously thin, appearing to be the same one he had used to write each and every one of their parts for the song they had just played.

"Well, you see, that was a song I kind of just... wrote. To be played with a guitar. And I have someone I wanted to play it with. Oh, and, yeah, I have the part written out for the guitar too. I'm not sure I want to perform it in an ensemble like this..." Cindy replied to him, turning him down and sounding apologetic for her refusal to contribute to the piece like she usually did when she drifted off of what was written in the original.

"Oh. Well, that's fine too. You can still perform with us, and I'll write in a new part here, then after we perform, we'll let your guitarist and you have a duet: how does that sound?" Mr. Grey asked her, now grinning at his offer, which he knew she couldn't turn down. Sometimes, he was just the best.

"That would be awesome. So, right after our performance... I'll start my duet at 5:45pm on Friday then?" Cindy asked him.

"Yes. Just get me the name of your guitarist and the name of your piece before then so I can put it into the schedule for the evening. You have a 10 minute time slot... is that enough?"

"That's more than enough, really. Maybe I'll talk about the piece a little before we perform it then. Thanks Mr. Grey. Really, thanks," Cindy said to him, as she handed him back his music and began to pack some of her things. The bell was going to ring soon.

"The piece is called Relentless Reminiscence."

The other instrumentalists replied to her announcement of the title with some *ooh's*, mocking her awkwardly emotional name for her song. But that was only to the title.

"And I'll be playing it with Damian Huong. H-u-o-n-g. Are you done writing that down?... Good. Yeah, he's my boyfriend, guys, and, in fact, it's our anniversary that day... so?" Cindy said in response to the snickering among some of the instrumentalists who knew her well, or who had seen her walking around with Damian before.

"Alright. Make sure both of you show up on time then."

"Don't worry, I will. Four years, guys," said Cindy, winking at some of her friends who had been in the group of instrumentalists who played with her.

She got up and walked out of the concert hall back into the school to get to her next class, not noticing Autumn Kizuno sitting at the back of the concert hall, in the top row of seats glaring down at her, jealousy radiating from every square inch of her body.

Chapter 22

Back on her street after running all the way across town, not even once looking back to catch a glimpse of the magnificent concert hall, standing tall and mocking her, she soon stood before her house.

Sure, there was no school, but she had had enough for the day.

Before walking in to her house, Autumn stood outside for a few seconds, looking at the large Kizuno residence. She knew it would never really be the same as their house in Tokyo. *Never.*

All their outdoor decorations had been poorly remade by her mother, as they couldn't bring everything they owned overseas with them.

She frowned at the thought of having to throw away and give away so much of their old belongings... the 28-coloured paper windmill she had made and hung on the side of their house, the paper flowers carefully drawn and coloured in, hours of time invested in the splendour of the makeshift petals.

Really, everything she missed held more sentimental value than physical value - but that just made it hurt even more.

She stepped into the small threshold of her family's porch, grazing her fingers lightly across the sun-warmed rosewood glimmering lightly to the shade of something almost like golden oak. It was a glistening tone to the lifeless support beams holding up the extended roof. The rosewood… it felt just like the same material his guitar was made of: the strong, firm body of it, polished, as she ran her fingers along the smooth neck… his neck…

She couldn't stand herself sometimes.

Pushing open the door, she stomped inside, her shoes left outside on her porch, on the doormat with everyone else's – but she didn't make it half way into the main hallway of her house before she stopped walking, and gazed in fear at what she saw before her.

Her mother - always strong at heart, complaining about anything that didn't go her way until it complied, reducing people in powerful positions to tears with her threats and her insults - was sitting at the table, clutching a piece of paper tightly, and crying.

It seemed like her mother's heart was pouring out of her eyes; that she was unable to hold it in no matter how hard she tried to. Making small noises deep within her throat, her mother didn't seem to want to be approached, nor did it seem like she noticed Autumn's entrance into the house, and Autumn was going to let her be and silently disappear up the stairs, when her mother called out loud to no one in particular.

"Drunk driver? What kind of insane idiot would get themselves, and all of them killed? Hm? I hadn't talked to them for years… didn't know where they lived. I hadn't met his children… I didn't even know he had them! And now… all of them, dead."

Autumn's mother became stiff, unmoving, her head down, staring straight at the news article set down on the living room table. Through her mother's fine black hair, she could see three or four pictures on the page, though any details were blocked out by the tresses flowing down her mother's head, obscuring the majority of the page.

Suddenly, her mother had stopped sobbing, stopped talking to herself, leaving everything silent.

Autumn didn't want to take a step or make a single move for fear of being heard by her mother and confronted. Her mother *was* in a vulnerable position, but that just made it so much scarier to imagine what her mother might do if she saw Autumn watching her.

A thought at the back of her mind pushed forth and told her to investigate the article when her mother moved to another location, probably towards the time her dad would be home with a new guest. But that was a strange thought too. *It must be serious if her mother stayed home.*

Her mother had soon gotten back to sobbing, calling out names of childhood friends she had back in Tokyo, school mates that both she and the deceased knew, speaking to herself about how they had known each other for so long, and hadn't seen each other since she had moved away. A few comprehensible words were "composition", "together", and "Chan", but those words didn't mean very much to Autumn.

With her mother loudly mourning again, Autumn snuck upstairs, her gentle footsteps up the last few remaining steps went undetected.

When she made it back to her room, she lay down on her bed, still careful not to create any sort of sound.

She felt fed up with how her day had gone, how life always seemed to turn out for her. Her drawing of pain had been overcome with too many sources, too many symbols that she could not visualize: her parents' usage of her as a possession, the feeling of creating something brilliant and never being willing to show anyone else, the sinking feeling of secret love gone wrong, with no solution.

She couldn't even draw pain properly.

If anyone had seen her at that moment, they would have noticed her eyes immediately, wide open and staring at the ceiling, debating whether or not to...

"Okay, so we'll just drop by the beach, and at 5:20 we need to start heading back to the concert hall? I know you have a performance, but why do I have to bring my guitar?" Damian asked Cindy, raising his eyebrows playfully in inquiry: he already knew that she had written yet another piece for them, one to mark their 4th year anniversary. In fact, he was pretty sure she already knew he knew, but before he managed to put in enough thought to confuse himself, Cindy replied.

"It's a surprise," she told him, smiling widely already, her eyes telling him that she already knew he was conscious of the fact that her surprise was entirely expected. "Oh stop laughing, you."

Damian dodged to the side, slowly, playfully dodging her finger as she attempted to poke him. "Alright, so, do you want to go back to my house now?"

"No, actually, my mom wants me home as soon as possible tonight. She says she's going to bring me to visit some of her friends up nearer to Grey Falls. It was something about renovations in their basement that they wanted a "young person's" opinion on. I think they want to start renting it out to some of the students at Grey Falls."

"But don't those friends live less than a kilometre away from where their daughter goes to univ-"

"Yeah, they do. I know right? They can be so annoying sometimes... my god. Anyway, I'll talk to you later tonight then. I'll ask to use their phone and call you, when they get into their talks about how much they've knit in the past week or something."

"Awesome. I'll look forward to it then. Have fun!" Damian said to her, chuckling lightly, hugging her warmly before she departed in the direction of her house, looking back and waving only once as he stood there, not quite ready to walk back to *his* house yet.

Hands in his pockets, he stood there idly, watching Cindy walk away, her long black hair blowing lightly in the gentle breeze. A quick flashback broke through his consciousness, and brought him back to the past for about a second.

"Bye, Damian..."

But that was over, and it wouldn't happen again. Four happy years together, and sure, they had their bumps and bruises along the long, long road, but he knew that they could both see the miles ahead of them that they would travel. *Together*.

Damian began to wonder though; he began to wonder about what had happened to *Autumn* after their confrontation yesterday.

In fact, he even wondered about what had happened *during* their confrontation... so many confusing aspects to life. He just assumed she'd get over him and move on... they had only talked for a day, after all.

He just assumed she would be fine.

Chapter 23

Lying awake in bed and unable to sleep, Autumn wondered how she could possibly make it to Thursday morning as she stared wide-eyed at her ceiling.

The night had brought darkness into her house, engulfing every square inch of it - the ceilings, the floors, the walls -with the black radiance of the later hours. The darkness had taken over her room, shutting out any and all light, except for the streetlights on outside, ever watching over everything in the vicinity. The darkness had also captured the rest of her house, putting her mother into the shadows in her room after dinner, the tears only a memory of the daylight, and the news article abandoned on the table in her living room.

The news article... it wasn't really of too much concern to Autumn, other than the fact that it piqued her interest, made her curious to know who this man was to her mother. She knew they had written several compositions together... several of which she'd had to play in the past, a lot of them extremely important to her mother – but Autumn had never had enough interest in the topic to ask her mother about anything. And now this man was dead.

Autumn sighed. Death always got around so quickly, ruining the happiness of so many, seizing the lives of so many, engulfing the world in its dark, cold grasp, just like when the sun sets at the end of the day.

Soon it was to be the end of the day for her, though.

She closed her eyes, thinking of all the darkness that had entered her life, for a moment completely ignoring her mother's pain, and everyone else's in the world. The only thing that had to matter to her at that time was herself. She thought, and she thought harder: where was her grandmother? Yes, she had passed away, was under her grave now, but truly, where *was* she?

Her grandmother, Hoshi Kizuno, a *hoshi* being a bright star in her night sky, the light that had guided Autumn through her darkness, now within the lifeless vice of Death himself.

So where was her light now? Who would tell her where to go?

Late into Wednesday night and Cindy was still up, not willing to go to bed without putting the absolute finishing touches on her composition. She had to be ready before the time came for them to perform together. She hoped Damian wouldn't screw up his part without seeing it before performing though: she considered what might happen, weighed the circumstances, and decided that it would really make things a lot more interesting.

With major editing, she ended up looking at her piece as a whole, looking at how the chords fit in, along with the construction of the different melodies and their sequences in the song. As she always did with her work, she had to have a distinct theme throughout her piece, though the only voices in the song were instruments, there was still a recurring aspect to the entire piece. From start to finish, at the beginning and endings of phrases, at the point of climax in every section of the melody, the tension would be created, or relieved, by her Cmaj9 chord.

The chord that she had built an entire song off of, that she had released upon her classmates, her co-workers in musical performance, when she had seen it. The trigger to the emotional and musical reservoirs within her held definite significance, and so, she gave it just that in her piece.

A chord - a culmination of several notes, each holding its own pitch, but still harmonious to each of the other ones, some notes more important than others, but never actually taking prominence. Each note was another sound to her, and each individual sound, the five notes, five words to be spoken by her instrument, were poetic to her ears.

The entire piece was originally harsh, an argument between the guitar and the piano, but towards the end, to the sound of those five familiar words, they resolve their argument, and have a pleasant exchange instead. The exchange was still shadowed though, by the feelings that forcefully occurred within their argument, the strings struck and picked by the two instruments, a high, light voice speaking with the deep, lower voice: the five words repeated over and over, in an attempt to bring things back to the way they were.

At the very start of the piece, things begin peacefully, a perfect opening, but they're tossed around, with the absence of the familiar phrase, the voices that carried the music along... and, though eventually the five notes return, they can't return things to exactly the way they were at the beginning.

C, E, G, B, D. Can't every girl be desired? The notes pounded words in to her head, the acronym not escaping her. Each note had something it wanted to say, and they were speaking to her, wondering how and why Autumn, that other girl, couldn't find someone else. Why *couldn't* she stay away from Damian and her? What was it that *had* gone on between Autumn and Damian?

A Fresh Beginning, finished except for the lyrics. He had all his notes written down, a melodic part clearly laid out before him, the notes ringing in his head even after he had set his guitar down beside him. The problem was, he had no words to put to his song.

He knew he could keep singing about his love, and how it was true, along with whatever other generic lyrics would come to his mind, but he knew this song had to be different. This one had to have more meaning behind it. He wanted to put his voice into the guitar, to speak with his notes instead of mindlessly making music that sounds good to other people.

In deciding that, it felt like instead of a composition, it was his notebook lying open before him. The musical notes on the page dissolved, melting off the page, leaving him with line after line of blank, cold paper.

Exerting all the effort that he could, looking long and hard at the flat surface, he didn't feel the words coming to him. He continued staring and staring, again reaching the point in his writing that he felt too tired to express himself. It made him feel frustrated, and he picked up his guitar again, looking for the solution.

Damian began to play his song again, each chord change a rapid movement of his fingers, humming a melodic line to his strumming, off beat, on beat; but he was still unable to put words to it. There were no words that *he* could sing to express his own emotions – but he had to, and he knew that as he continued to hold his pen over the paper with no words to write, that he needed to find some before the night was over.

Arms set down on the frigid desktop, fingers stiff and motionless, his bed called out to him, but he only longed for the words he needed to reply to it.

Chapter 24

Thursday morning, a mere one day from their fourth year anniversary, and Cindy was ecstatic. She rose with the sun that overly warm and humid morning, and shined just like the brightest star in their galaxy, glimmering brightly even as she washed the sleep off of her eyes in the bathroom.

They had a performance the next day that they would be doing together, finally showing the world how close they were as they played their instruments together, letting everyone see their musical abilities, and also letting everybody know about them. *Them, the two of them, still together after four years.*

She didn't want to have Damian embarrass himself by playing something incorrectly though, and she planned on making it so that he would have some time in advance, and not have to sight-read during the performance: already sitting on her desk was another copy of the score, the guitar part and the piano part photocopied onto another page of off-white, cream-coloured paper.

Looking over the two copies of the same composition, she considered this anomaly and others that had showed up recently. These two compositions, one of the same, were two parts of the whole. One looked and sounded ridiculous by itself with long bouts of silence and odd notes here and there, and so the composition could only be considered to be wonderful, a work of art, when put together. Again, she was thinking of the two voices of their instruments, the piano, the guitar, to be speaking to each other on-stage, in front of hundreds of people in the small, cozy town of Perten... nearly half the people in the town would know to show up to the performance.

Sweat beaded up on her forehead as she anticipated the sharp movements of the piece, a curve of notes from one melody in to the next, the chaotic frenzies of notes only adding to the beauty of it all. Contrast was a major factor to this piece, and she couldn't wait to see how it all turned out. Still, she couldn't help but wonder if the people might not like it.

Cindy stuffed all of her books and the two copies of her composition in to her small, beige book bag, and closed the flap, running her fingers along the smooth surface of the hand-sewn bag, bought from China years ago, brought back by her father... her father who was now buried under his grave, North of Perten, joining all the other souls who had been snatched by death.

She could still remember when she was a child, always going to her father for everything, as she had never been fond of her mother: her mother had always yelled at her, blaming every little bad thing on her, and her father would be the one to come to her rescue.

She could still remember...

All those days her father brought her down to the park, pushed her on the swings, waited for her at the bottom of the slide, a happily smiling man's face always happily there for her, smiling joyfully wherever she went.

She could still remember...

When her father had brought her to school for the first time ever in Kindergarten and how she had been the only child not to cry in the strange new environment of the classroom, feeling perfectly secure with her dad, trusting him every step of the way.

She could still remember...

156

Finishing Kindergarten and considering all the job opportunities she had in her childish fantasies: a ballerina, a princess, maybe a firefighter. And her dad had still been there for her the whole time. After a long hard day of colouring, or walking to music class to watch her silly teacher clap rhythms for them, her day started and ended with her father, all the time.

She could still remember...

During a day in her second month of first grade, on her way home from another day of school, her father happily whistled and took a moment to look in the rear view mirror, checking up on his little princess, Cindy smiling happily back at him...

The wind shield shattered as an SUV zoomed in their path and destroyed the front half of the vehicle not one kilometre back into the city. She could still remember the yellow fluorescent tape everywhere, her mother crying, but still trying to assure her that everything would be alright, that things would be just fine... but they weren't.

She could still remember.

Suddenly, Cindy was clutching the bag to her chest, almost hoping to bring her father back, caressing it gently, not letting it go. It was all she had left of him.

Thursday morning was only a dreary beginning to the hours to come before he could go back to sleep, the same as any other day for Damian. His eyes begged for him to let them close and fall back to sleep, but it was already 7:12am, and he didn't have the time to crawl back into his bed after he had taken a full 12 minutes to stand up and get out of it.

If it wasn't for Cindy, and the fact that he knew he had to get to school, he probably *would* have fallen right back to sleep.

That was the outcome of a mere three hours of sleep, so he found it impressive really, how it had *only* taken him 12 minutes: normally he'd have just slammed his hand downwards on the alarm clock and fallen back asleep, waiting for his dad to come push him out of bed, opening the curtains and waking him up in a want-to-be-young-again fashion. Oh, the horrors of it all.

A quick peek at his desk, to his song, perhaps in useless hope that words would have appeared over the lines of his melody on his song, the page still gaped openly back at him, no changes from the previous night. There were still no lyrics for him to sing when he played the song for Cindy on Friday, only one day away... he was disappointed with himself. The instrumental part itself would have to suffice though: there was no time left. Cindy had plans for them after school: but as to where they were going, she still hadn't told him.

Packing his bag for the fourth time that week, it was the unbreakable routine of his that he had to stick to, as it was something he had to do, and had constantly done for the last multiple years of his life. School was basically waking up, packing his bag, unpacking it, learning, falling asleep, and then repeating the process.

The tedium of everyday life was getting to his head, but he knew that he and "routine" were best friends, and they held on to each other for dear life. Anything outside of a schedule just didn't seem to want to end up happening for him.

His disappointment of a song sat on his desk as he walked down his house's stairs to eat his breakfast and prepare for the day ahead of him with Cindy... and the next day. That *would* definitely be something to look forward to – if he didn't feel like falling over any second from exhaustion.

Thursday morning, and there was only one day left until she would have to face them being together on stage. After her eavesdropping scenario the previous day when she was off school, and after Cindy had left, she had walked down towards the stage slowly, catching the attention of Mr. Grey as a visitor who had just entered the building. She then asked him the question that she knew the answer to. She asked if the concert hall was free on Friday, at around 5:00pm, so that she could practice, and the flustered man had apologized profusely to her, telling her that it was booked out by the school itself for an important performance, and that she could come back next week if she wanted to, and he could guarantee her a spot.

After Autumn re-assured him that writing her name down to return the week after was unnecessary, she left the building.

Autumn wasn't planning on going back the next week, in fact, she wasn't really planning on going anywhere. She had a plan: she would watch their performance, not draw any attention to herself, and then just end it all as she watched them. She wasn't sure if she was thinking correctly when she considered it, but she knew she had to do it.

There were too many things in Autumn's life that pressured her from every direction: her mother yelling at her about piano, but in secret crying about something she wouldn't share with anyone else; her heart pressuring her about Damian, her unrequited love never to be returned to her, a hopeless cause in all actuality; and finally, there was the pressure coming *from* Damian – she had recognized that look on his face when he had snapped out of his daze the other day, and looked right at her. He wanted her out of his life, and there was nothing she could really do about what he wanted.

To finish off her life in style, she had begun a picture, a simple sketch of a rope dangling down from the edge of a mountain, the precarious balance of all her emotions, on the verge of falling off, held by a single rope of sanity. That rope though, was breaking along the middle, slowly being torn apart by other forces, invisible to anyone else looking at her picture, but she knew they were there, tearing at the rope, her sanity - and so, it all ended up hanging on a single thread.

She was going to give up though, as she couldn't just sit there and wait for something else to cut the rope and send her hurtling over the brink of insanity... she would cut it herself, and in that thought, she knew she had her escape ready. Her escape was a knife: the same knife her grandmother had always used to cook the warm meals they shared together when she was young, not in Perten, but in Tokyo. It was always kept sharp, ready to slice meat and help scoop it up to be thrown into a pan to be cooked.

That knife which she had taken from her grandmother's room, from among Hoshi Kizuno's old possessions, and hidden, before the rest of her family could discard of everything like they had with all of the other old things in her grandmother's room. She couldn't let them throw away all she had left of her grandmother, so she kept that tiny piece of her favourite family member.

And that small piece of her grandmother would soon reunite them, when Autumn would commit the ultimate act of selfishness, or so she always read.

Autumn didn't care about her mother or anyone else at that moment though: it was time to be selfish for once and give up on the dependence of others.

The cold metal blade of the knife felt heavy in her bag, and she set it down by her doorway, shedding a single tear of remorse, knowing that Friday, the day she would see the true beauty of the love between Cindy and Damian, would be her last day.

Chapter 25

The simultaneous ringing of the bell and the sound from within his head were dissonant to each other, causing a nearly head-splitting headache in Damian's mind, but he had to bear with it. Cindy, oblivious to the fact that Damian had the same amount of sleep as she had, had nonetheless suggested they go back to his house to work, though it was clear that she had noticed his pain when they were about half way there.

They were walking to his house with minimal discussion, the first word being spoken by Cindy, asking about how Damian's chemistry class had gone, to which he replied with a groan of pain.

Cindy suddenly became extremely concerned, until he waved it off nonchalantly, not wanting her to get overly anxious about his headache. If there was one thing he *didn't* want when he was suffering from any sort of pain, it was attention from others to the pain he was suffering from.

By the time the couple reached his house, Damian was clutching his head, and Cindy was pushing herself to the limits of her mental ability not to rush him to some sort of aid or attempting to support him in some way, though she knew there was no way her skinny body was going to hold him up. She didn't like seeing him in pain though, even if there was nothing she could do to fix it. She wished they could just get to his house a bit faster. Tylenol awaited them.

Damian dizzily reached into his front-right pant pocket and attempted to find his keys, but they weren't there. Not wanting to search his backpack for the key, though he was pretty sure it would be there as he had left it there that morning, he continued to look in his pocket for something he knew wasn't there.

In the process of his search, his fingers grazed across something small: a piece of paper that felt like it had been ripped off of a larger piece of paper.

Damian wondered what it could be as his hands continued to search the bottoms of his deep jean pockets – but he realized what it was long before he gave up his search in his pockets, remembering the day he had walked outside bare-foot with his guitar. Autumn's phone number, still warm with her touch, was in his hand, and he clenched it tightly, once, before pulling it out subtly and letting it go. He didn't need to think about it anymore.

Cindy was lightly tapping her foot on the ground to a slow beat; she was mocking impatience, though Damian knew that she felt like they had all the time in the world whenever they were together. That was how he felt when he was with her at least.

Nevertheless, he let his bag down from his shoulder, and opened the flap, retrieving the small metal key from a side pocket. The jagged teeth of the key were his only way into his house, as his dad was out again. He inserted the key into the keyhole, and turned it.

He opened the door, waving his arm towards the interior of his home, welcoming Cindy, as he did basically every time she was over. Also, he was beckoning for her to go into the door before he did.

She walked in, casually slipping off her shoes and leaving them neatly on the doormat, walking in to his kitchen and beginning to search through his medicine cabinets for any sort of medicine that would help him with his headache. She fumbled with the various boxes, the bottles of pills, and finally uncovered a few samples of Tylenol.

Pouring a glass of cold water and passing it to Damian, Cindy told him to take it.

"You need to have some. I don't want you passing out suddenly if we go anywhere. If you don't take it, we'll just stay here all night, in your kitchen" Cindy warned him, knowing that he'd probably comply right after she said that.

"Fine."

Cindy was right.

First taking a sip of the tap water to wash out his dry mouth and get some moisture back into his throat, he swallowed the pill immediately afterwards, letting another mouthful of cold water rush through his system, hoping the effects of the pill would set in soon.

Damian gripped the table tightly, hoping to bring focus back to the world and stop it from spinning out of control, but gave up.

Sitting down, Damian settled his head down on his arms, the bottom of his chin pressed in to the cold marble countertop, and he exhaled deeply, shutting his eyes tightly as he did so. Cindy took that to mean that they might have to stay at his house for a while longer.

After nearly ten minutes of absolute silence, Damian raised his head, letting out a tiny sigh.

"How about we go upstairs now? Then we can go in about 20 minutes. You want me to bring my guitar, right?" Damian finally spoke, his tone even, seemingly feeling slightly better from his headache.

"Are you sure you're feeling better? I don't mind waiting at your house for a while longer... it's barely even three yet: we have time," Cindy replied, concern filling her voice.

"Yes, I'm absolutely sure I'm fine. Let's go upstairs."

Cindy complied, and they both got out of the kitchen chairs around the table, beginning to walk up the stairs to Damian's room.

Upon entering, Damian walked over to his desk, and stared at his composition with no lyrics, finally prepared to show Cindy, even though it was the day before their anniversary. She was allowed to know beforehand.

Seeing the sheet of music, Cindy knew immediately that it was a song that she had never heard before, that he had written yet another one for her, and she smiled. Pretty soon though, she had noticed the same thing he was fretting over: there were no lyrics anywhere on the pages.

"You know that sometimes, there's music you write that's just impossible to express with words? You can get your feelings in to the notes, in to your rhythms, the volume and the articulation of the notes... but you just can't find actual words to put to it. And, when times like that come up, you really don't have anything to worry about, Damian. This is absolutely beautiful with, or without lyrics..." Cindy told him.

A genuine smile flashed across her face, brightening up the room in an instant and making Damian feel better about his song being a failure of sorts.

"I'll play it for you then..."

"No, we'll wait until tomorrow. Don't worry, it can still be a surprise. That can be our little secret."

The two talked for a few more minutes about English, slow conversation about school work, until Cindy checked the time and changed the topic, saying to Damian, "Grab your guitar and let's go, if you're ready..."

Damian felt a lot better from his headache from earlier, and was ready to leave.

"Alright. Let's go. Off to the concert hall then," Damian replied, picking up his guitar and putting his bag over his back again. "We don't want to keep Mr. Grey waiting, right?"

Her life had spun out of control, and she didn't really know how to stop it. Well, she did, but she didn't. The knife was still in her bag, and she knew she wouldn't take it out until Friday, the next day... but then it would be the last time she did anything, really.

Wouldn't it be smarter to find some other way to resolve her life though? She could talk to someone... maybe even confront Damian again, but in a less accusatory fashion. There were endless possibilities that came to her mind at that moment, and Autumn was momentarily blinded by reason - the fact that she didn't *have* to use her knife at all wasn't fully sinking in though.

The thought of Damian drove a pain deep into her chest, and she clutched herself tightly, losing sight of what she could do instead of what she was planning, and once again blindly thinking of how she would end her life after watching Damian perform one last time: it was a private performance by him, just for her, or so it seemed.

Autumn's final picture, her rope dangling downwards with no beginning or end, but nearly broken down the middle, was sitting unframed on the top of her desk.

The precarious balance of her emotions outweighed all traces of sanity she felt that she still had – she couldn't do anything but let go of the rope or cut it at that point, then face the fall either way. The only difference was that with one option, she wasn't expecting it.

Her thoughts were driving her mad, as she looked at her rope hanging loosely from the top of the sketch paper that she had ripped out of her sketch pad and set on top of it..

Before she left the Earth to go find her grandmother, there were a few things she wanted to do. She knew she was still sane, holding on to the single thread of sanity she still had, resisting the push of *in*sanity.

Autumn felt that she was still a girl with wishes and dreams. There were still a few more things she wanted to do before...

She wanted to show her art to someone else, for one, as no one had ever seen the art that she had put so much time into, at least not since her family had moved to Perten: there was no one who cared enough that she would bother to show her drawings, her emotions put on paper. She wasn't sure if she could though. *No*, she *had* to. She would leave her sketch pad downstairs with a note to her mother before she left for school the next day in the morning, knowing full well that she would never get to walk through her own house's front door again. She would let her mother have that at least, a faint memory of the child she didn't care for.

Another thing she wanted was to play the piano in the concert hall by Perten Senior High. The majestic, brazen, grand piano in the centre of the stage there lured her towards it, made her want to be in its midst; she wanted to play it so very badly. Each and every single key of the beautiful instrument was calling out to her, telling her to stroke them, to strike them, and to remember what the piano was like back when she still lived in Tokyo. Each and every white and black key had a different pitch, a different memory hidden in each of their frequencies, awaiting the chance to arise and have Autumn linger upon them. She might do that tomorrow, if she got there early, before...

She hadn't practiced her piano in the last few days, as the sound of the light hammering of strings within the

166

magnificent instrument only made her detest it more than she already did.

The music that her mother had put so much care in to writing, and took so much pride in... she refused to play it anymore.

What did *she get from playing it for her mother? She got yelled at for not doing it well enough, that's what.*

Autumn's mouth was hanging open as she thought though, and she felt as if there was something on the tip of her tongue that she had to say: something that absolutely couldn't wait. She couldn't figure out what it was though, that she had to say.

Trying to close her mouth, she suddenly whispered to herself under some sort of strange impulse within her.

"Why not...?" she asked herself, an incomplete question. Whatever the rest of it was going to be was muffled by the closing of her soft lips together, sealing away the words that would save her from fate.

Chapter 26

Thursday afternoon: Cindy and Damian were together in the concert hall, and Damian's headache had gone away for the most part, a faint pounding in the back of his head the only remnant of his lack of sleep. Bothersome, but not painful any longer.

His guitar was in his hand: he had never put it in to a case before, nor did he actually have one. The rounded edges of the guitar were still undamaged though, as he constantly kept it in good condition, setting it down carefully and paying full attention to how he was handling it while bringing it around with him to places.

The neck of the guitar was warm with his grip, but the metal strings were still cold, waiting for him to play them, to make music with them. It felt invigorating to have the instrument in his hand, and he was finally able to completely ignore the constant throbbing in his head. He wanted to sit up on the stage, to close his eyes and imagine the audience waiting in suspense for his fingers to come in contact with the strings, to dazzle them with his exquisite skills.

"Okay, here's the piece I wrote for… us. Don't laugh, please… well, I know you won't, but still. I called it *Relentless Reminiscence*. So… what do you think?" Cindy asked Damian meekly as she passed him a copy of her new composition, snapping him right back to reality. She didn't notice though, as she looked away, afraid to check and see what his reaction would be.

Damian took the four pages and set them down on a stand with extensions in front of him, again taking the time to appreciate the fact that Cindy kept all her notes on harmonizing her chords on each of her pieces. It let him see and feel how the music would sound before he even played it.

It also made him feel slightly smarter every time he could read and understand the harmony in a piece. He liked that.

Suddenly feeling very awkward just staring at the composition, and not wanting to judge something without actually listening to it, for fear that Cindy would assume he was just saying it sounded good to be polite to her, he sat down and rested his guitar on his thigh.

Rubbing his finger tips quickly before setting them down on the frets of the guitar, Damian began to play the piece, starting right from the beginning, even though he was just background to what she would be playing.

The familiar chords were there, the ones that Cindy almost always used in her piece, and her signature sequences were present, with a D Phrygian scale, yet another mark she left on all of her music. After about half a minute, he had finally reached his part, the melody, when he picked up the pace of the piece and kicked it into the next gear.

His sight-reading was slightly rusty, as it had been months since he had last played one of Cindy's pieces, and he feared he would mess up, but he still pressed on. His fingers were a blur, frantically moving up and down his strings, and the occasional screeching of his skin against the metal rang through the dense area on the stage – Cindy never failed to push him to the limits of his skill, but never let him say that something was too hard. *He loved the fear of reading a piece hard enough that he might mess up while playing it.*

At that point in the song, Cindy had joined in, walking over to the piano, silently running her fingers over the keys before playing the harmonic part to the melody, only there to give voice to his notes. She was supporting him, the only thing keeping him going, on time, and she was perfectly in tune with him.

In synchronicity, they finished the piece together, hurtling through the notes as if there was no tomorrow, finally bowing and clapping to each other, smiling like a pair of idiots.

At least they were happy idiots.

"I like it," said Damian, smiling at Cindy, attempting to cure her of the insecurity she had in every piece she wrote.

"Thanks..." she replied, walking over and hugging him, only giving him about three seconds of warning to set his guitar down on the hardwood stage. He put his arms around her and held her close to him, not wanting to let go.

"I have something to show you, Cindy... just give me a minute to get it out of..." breaking the hug, Damian had cut himself off half way through his sentence to turn around in his chair to pick up his bag and rummage through it. He pulled out his notebook and set it down on his lap, closed, the cover facing both of them, happily twinkling in the light of the dim spotlights above.

"I have a feeling you already know what it is, but, still. I want to show you all of it. My poetry... and some other stuff nearer to the beginning... we'll go back in time right now, just you and me," Damian offered her, opening up to the most recent page, containing a poem titled "Dissipate".

> With you lying in my arms,
> The world dissolves around us,
> There is nothing else that exists,
> It's only you, me,
> And the love between us.

170

And when you're not here,
I miss you,
Wish you could be here with me,
And calm my heart,
As it aches for you.

It seems an eternity,
Before I can see you again,
Weeks and weeks of unbearable longing,
Seems like we're separated by oceans,
Miles and miles of insurmountable distance.

But right now,
With you lying in my arms,
As the world dissolves around us,
There is only you, me,
And the love between us.

Damian read the entire poem out to Cindy, and she was nearly crying with joy by the end of it. "I love you, Damian. Thank you... you always seem to know what to do..."

"I love you too," he responded to her, "Well of course I do!" He was winking at her, as he flipped back to the poem from the day before that. In that moment, and as they continued to whisk the night away in musical harmony, he knew that the only things that existed on the stage were Cindy, him, and the love between them, as he felt the word dissolve around them.

Standing in the clearing off the shore of Grey Falls, Cindy and Autumn were sitting next to each other, happily carving words and pictures in to the ground, both with knives in hand, leaving their own marks on the Earth, tiny and insignificant stains in nature. Damian walked by them, singing as he played a song on his guitar, the lyrical notes ringing in all of their ears.

He stopped by, and sat down on a tree stump, the remnants of a tree that had been recently cut down, and he strummed away to them, as they all put aside their indifferences and sang along to his song...

Then, Autumn woke up from her dream, seeing the alarm's LCD display flashing a red "9:45pm" at her eyes. She didn't recall falling asleep, but she was suddenly terrified of how abstract her dream was. She swore it was her brain attempting to tear her apart; whenever she did, heard, or saw something, she always thought it had to have a reason behind it.

Autumn's head started hurting as she tried to figure out what she had just dreamt.

Sweat dripped off of her forehead, landing on the cool bed sheets.

She walked over to the air conditioner and turned it up a bit, hoping to get back to bed soon, which would be impossible if she kept getting warmer. Hearing the motor of the machine turn faster and feeling the physical decrease in temperature, she wondered what would happen when her cold, lifeless body was found in the concert hall... would anyone care?

Who would be the first to see her?

Chapter 27

Struggling to let go of him, not wanting to wait until the next day to see him again, Cindy finally relinquished her tight grip around Damian's body. The embrace felt much too short, as she kissed him lightly on the lips and had to turn around and open her front door.

Even after she entered and closed the door behind her, looking in to his eyes for one last time before they would depart, not to see each other again until the next morning, she could taste him on her lips and feel his touch on her skin. She wanted more of it, and suddenly knew how many of the other girls at school felt when they looked at him, feeling very protective of her boyfriend of four years suddenly. It didn't feel too bad, really.

Playing the piece with Damian hadn't gone too badly, and he seemed to like it. At least, it didn't seem like he was lying when he offered his opinion on the music she had written for them. The music didn't seem all that important when she suddenly remembered something she should have remembered earlier, but hadn't. The music could wait, but she felt the absolute need to check on the other thing right at that moment.

Rushing up the stairs and in to her room, Cindy yelled out a loud, ubiquitous "hey Mom!" to the large house, not wanting to be accosted by her mother for not having the manners to greet her "superiors" upon "arriving at her destination." She just loved her mother's phrasing at some times, when her broken English and direct translation from Chinese got the better of her.

Walking through the door of her room, the doorframe the gateway in to the only paradise of her house: it was both solemn and solitary, confined and contriving, the presence of her piano inspirational to creation, and the sound-proofed walls offering her the daily opportunity to shut herself out from the world. Always a pleasure to be in there, her reason for going to her room that minute was not to relax, but to search.

On her knees, Cindy began to dig through her closet, causing a tumult of fabrics, tossing around loose articles of clothing, taking down giant containers filled with clothes that didn't fit her anymore. She scoured the floor of the dark abyss of outfits, wondering where it might be.

The anticipation burnt in her mind, and she continued to await the moment her fingers would brush against the small box she had hidden so many months ago, in preparation for their 4th year together.

So many old pieces of clothing, articles she knew she hadn't worn in years, and that she knew she would never wear again. Just memories that she would never revisit, piled on top of each other, smothering out the present and forcing her to dig through all of it to find what she was looking for.

Still not finding it, she stood up to take a second and stretch her back and dust off her hands a bit, clapping them together once, then twice. Standing up tall, she looked at the hopeless pile of clothes and caught sight of something dangling from above, hidden towards the back of everything.

It was a black dress that went slightly past her knees, and was open-backed with a dangerous neckline, that she would no longer feel comfortable wearing in public... but that wasn't a problem the last time she wore it: only one day off of exactly four years ago. The day they began dating, the day that Damian had finally gathered up the nerve to ask her the question... she still remembered it so very distinctly.

Giving up on the search for the time being, she took a minute to reminisce; a momentary break from her frantic hunt.

Nervous, her legs were shaking a tiny bit as she walked into George's Café. She had never been in the place before, but it seemed nice enough. There were a few outlandish frescoes hanging around and the lamps were a bit too "retro" for her style, but it appeared to be quite a cozy little place.

Cindy nearly jumped out of her skin as the bells hanging over the door signalled her entry to the store: an assault of loud noise the moment she walked in to a place she was unfamiliar with was not what she wanted to be welcomed with. Still shuddering slightly from the shock, she looked upwards and glared briefly at the bells, satisfactory iniquity leaking through her gaze. Hopefully the bells felt her pain.

Done with getting her revenge on the bells hanging over the door, she looked downwards, scanning the café and realizing suddenly that it was almost entirely empty. The only occupant at any of the tables was...

Cindy began to blush furiously, the shade of her cheeks flying down the colour wheel, landing right on a full shade of cherry red, giving her the look of being out in the cold for too long, even though the temperature outside was well over 20 degrees Celsius, even at four in the afternoon. Damian smiled at her shyly, and she was obliged to respond with the same expression, though slightly abashed by her confrontation with the bells.

"So... you're already here. Umm... am I late?" Cindy asked him meekly, holding back, afraid to say something wrong and have him stare at her awkwardly and walk away from her.

She was 14, not even in high school yet, but she felt bad about her social status all the time: 14 full years into her life, and she had never been asked out on a date by a guy – up until now. She didn't want to mess anything up.

"No, of course not... you're just in time. I just got here early. It's alright, because I know George. That's him right there... he's the only one who works here, by the way. Family friend of mine... really nice guy, actually. He let me book the entire place, just for us," Damian replied to Cindy, speaking eloquently, but still smiling politely at her.

"Oh... that's cool then. So... what's up?" Cindy asked him, feeling a sudden lack of things to talk about.

"You play piano, right?..."

Damian was the one who sparked the topic, the common ground that they held with each other; they continued talking about music for the remainder of their hour together. Cindy had to get home before 5:00pm as she wasn't allowed out after that. The curfew of an 8th grader made her sigh in exasperation whenever she got home at 5:01pm, or even worse, 5:02pm. Off to the world of hour-long speeches about the potential dangers of the dark.

Cindy had so many questions for him, about his guitar, about his interests in music, how much he knew, and she knew that he was perfect for her. When their hour was up, Damian had asked her the question, the words she had been waiting for all afternoon long.

"Cindy... umm... I know it's really kind of sudden, but I like you a lot and I was wondering... will you go out with me?" Damian asked, the question coming out as shyly as her first hello.

"Yes... I'll go out with you," Cindy replied to him after about two seconds of pretended deliberation, "I'll see you on Monday then, okay?"

"Alright," Damian said, looking vaguely surprised, as if he hadn't expected her to say "yes", as if he was thinking that the whole date had been a waste of time, a lost cause.

"Good night," Cindy said, before quickly rushing out, hoping to make it back home before the clock struck five when her mother would unleash the fury of a concerned parent on her.

Damian waved goodbye to her very slightly, still in shock as he watched her leave the café.

The end of her recollection of that afternoon brought her back to current time. And her current dilemma.

Cindy got on her knees yet again and dove back into her closet, pushing aside the masses of shirts and pants, suddenly considering the fact that she may have lost it, discarded it… but she had to hope it was still in there as she kept looking.

A promise ring, nothing too fancy, but it was still silver, with their names engraved into the interior of the band, with two entwined vines shaped on the front of the ring, symbolic to their ties together, and how close they were. Symbolic of how breaking them apart from each other was to sever them both.

She had bought it in preparation for their fourth anniversary, then kept the pair of rings in their original box, and locked them in a sort of metal time capsule. Knowing the key was hidden inside her piano, she would retrieve it soon, but she still had to find the small metal container first.

Rounding the corner of her closet door, she continued to search the bottom of the endless pit of clothing, brushing along the dusty floor, never knowing that the floor space inside was so dirty: she would need to get some of her clothes washed then put away, soon.

She felt her heart skip a beat, and nearly stop, when she reached the end of the soft mass of clothing, and her finger came in contact with the cold metal surface of the container.

Reaching her hand in a tiny bit further, she encompassed the entire case - nearly the size of a can of pop - in her grasp and pulled it out of the closet into full view.

Though it was covered in dust, the place her hands had just touched allowed the light to shine on the container and show Cindy the familiar silver shade of it; the last glimmer of it she had seen was when she had put it away.

The treasure she thought she had lost, left there from so long ago - and she had found it.

Holding the container to her chest (after wiping off the remnants of the dust with a tissue from the tissue box on her desk), she approached her upright piano and opened the top. Reaching her hand in, careful not to touch any of the strings, she already saw what she was looking for. Closing her fingers around the small metal teeth, she extracted the miniature key from the depths of the piano and felt the cold bite of it in the palm of her hand.

Holding the two items in each of her hands, she looked at them for a second, mulling over her thoughts of what she was thinking as she had come up with the idea of these rings. Her heart beat quickly, the excitement at finally seeing a ring on her finger, and the other on his, was overwhelming.

She unlocked the container, and emptied the contents in to her hand: there were the two boxes for the two rings... and a note in her handwriting, written to herself.

Chapter 28

Finally, the day had come, and Autumn started questioning herself. Would she be able to bring herself to do it? This was the last time she would see her room, if she left it. The last time she would be able to touch the soft, velvety bed sheets made for her by her grandmother. The last time she would see her old curtains, the books she owned on her shelf, her collection of original manga in Japanese. The last time she would smell the light perfumed scent her mother left as she passed through the hallways, the musk left in the upstairs bathroom by her father before he left for work every morning. It would be the last time she walked down the stairs, rounded each bend in the steps, the last time she would wave goodbye to her mother after she had her breakfast made for her, the last time she would eat breakfast at her family's antique table. Soon, it would be the last time she saw, heard, smelt, tasted, or felt anything.

It was selfish, but she had already relinquished that thought: it didn't matter how selfish she was being when she did this. Autumn couldn't bring herself to torture her mother like that though... and she still had things she had to fulfill before she could...

She had brought her filled sketch pad down to the living room with her, and was now sitting in the same seat her mother had sat at when she had put her head down and cried for the death of Mr. Chan. Her last words to any member of her family had to be spoken through pen and paper; her final wave at her mother seemed like it wasn't enough, and she felt for a second that she wouldn't be able to let go... to cut her rope... but she looked at her note again.

Dear Mother,

I'm sincerely sorry for doing this, but I absolutely had to leave. No, I haven't run away from home... I can't come back from where I'm going. I'm with grandma now, and she'll watch over me: don't worry. I'm not going to request you not shame me for what I've done, as I know how you probably feel about it, but I just couldn't take it anymore.

This is a pad of drawings that I've been keeping for a while now, though I haven't shown you any of *these* ones. They were too private... but now I have no secrets from you, or the rest of the world.

I love you Mom, goodbye, and I'm sorry. Please tell father the same...

Good luck to you both in your future ventures,

Autumn Kizuno

The words, she knew, would haunt her mother for a while to come, and they would never leave her mind, pestering her to the point of insanity, a constant nagging voice in the back of her mind. The voice would ask her questions – questions about why she hadn't raised her daughter better, why she had let this happen. Then her mother would know.

Now that she could show someone else her art, though it was only her mother, she knew all of her drawings would be looked at, and investigated deeply for any source of a reason behind her... end.

With still one goal to finish, she ate her last meal, the toast drifting solidly down her throat. Even after she had washed it down with a glass of cold orange juice, the condensation dripping down the sides, the lump in her throat still remained. Copious amounts of irritation were rolling over her, and she shut her eyes, trying to shake it all off.

She wanted to visit the piano of her past quickly, before school started, so she set off immediately, not wanting to be late for class, even if it *was* to be her last day. Autumn really didn't want to end on a bad note with anyone. And she just wanted a glimpse of the keys, maybe run her fingers along the faux ivory… it would be enough for her.

A few more hours and they would be together for the entire night, together in the concert hall, together on the stage, together in their music. Cindy couldn't wait until when she would see Damian, and they could celebrate their four long years together, that had seemed like almost no time at all.

After showering quickly in the morning, as she usually did so that her long hair didn't have to be flat, Cindy put on some of the clothes she didn't consider modest enough to be "work clothes", but not flashy enough to be "dress clothes".

They were her performance clothes: a tight black skirt that reached slightly past her knees, a white dress shirt, and her half inch heels. They made her seem sophisticated, and when the whole thing was combined with her dim shade of red lipstick with minimal make up elsewhere, she looked quite professional indeed.

Cindy glanced over at her bathroom table, off to the side and a safe distance away from the sink and the garbage can. She ran her eyes briefly over the two finely shaped rings, resting motionlessly in their open boxes. She couldn't wait to present Damian with them only a few hours from then.

She smiled, happily looking at herself in the mirror, knowing how many people would see her like that later, including her own mother, Damian's father, all of her friends, their parents, her teachers... nearly everyone she knew. They would all be dazzled by her – Cindy was only taking a moment to be conceited: she needed to do it more often.

Going over the list of people she knew were showing up for sure later that night, she was absent-mindedly straightening her pages, knocking their bottoms on her desk before putting them into a folder that she would stick in to her backpack, next to all of her textbooks.

Suddenly, a cold shiver ran down her back as she thought of one final person who might show up for the performance who she hadn't thought of until that moment: Autumn.

The time had almost come for their 4th year anniversary, and Damian was wiping himself off after a brief cold shower to make himself seem cleaner in his performance attire. He couldn't wait to see Cindy.

The words he would say to her were already running themselves over in his mind, as he was thinking of how to phrase what he wanted to tell her, phrasing and re-phrasing while looking in the mirror and absent-mindedly checking his hair, making sure every strand was in place.

"Cindy, I love you, and I want to tell you... show you how much the last four years have meant to me. Umm... I want to, I *really* want to let you see... let you know how the last four years we spent together... with each other... no, together, have meant to me... Awgh! What do I say?" Damian shut his eyes, thinking hard as to what it was that he wanted to tell her.

It was probably better than if he had tried to come up with something to say the previous day though: he didn't have a headache.

Damian sighed, suddenly considering the fact that letting what he said be natural was better than planning something ahead of time that he would most likely end up sounding stupid saying to her. It just needed to mean something when he said it to her – that made him feel slightly better about how he didn't know exactly what he wanted to say.

The day had finally come after the long hours awaiting it in the days preceding it. Finally, he could say that he'd loved Cindy for a full four years, and that they had lived it together. He could perform with her that night, and after that, they could go, be free, and have the entire night to themselves.

All that was left for him to do was to last the entire day in his uncomfortable shirt and dress pants, ignore the pain of his toes being pushed together by his too-small dress shoes, and then perform a song he couldn't play all that well in front of a large audience.

He would get to humiliate himself by playing multiple wrong notes, and getting lost in the piece, but Cindy would probably save him from that in the end also. At least he would get that tiny amount of time to spend with Cindy afterwards, and the whole stressful experience would be in celebration with each other: that was all that mattered.

A full 20 minutes before any bell in the town rang announcing the start of school, the concert hall in front of Perten Senior High was still deserted when Autumn arrived, rounding the last corner and entering the empty building.

Opening the outside door, which, surprisingly enough, had been left unlocked, she entered the pitch black concert hall, feeling around the sides of the wall for some sort of light switch, but not succeeding. Autumn was forced to resort to drastic measures, as she reached in to one of the side compartments in her backpack and pulled out a small flash light she kept to read in the dark whenever she got the chance: it would be the only thing able to guide her down the treacherous steps in the complete darkness.

The dim light from the door remained, and shined around the walls and the floors of the building that found themselves in the direct path of the outside.

Taking a step away from the door, it closed behind her, a final thud, leaving her unable to see metres in front of her.

Autumn was left to use her flashlight that shined its faint light wherever she directed it, though she couldn't see much from where she was standing: still by the outside door, at the top of the stairs that led down to the centre, the stage.

The concert hall made her feel as if she was completely cut off from the rest of the world, the only things in sight were the steps directly in front of her, as the building lacked any windows. Lightly placing one foot in front of the other and descending towards the stage, each step she took emitted a booming echo; the acoustics of the concert hall were amazing.

Though the anonymity of the darkness, and not being able to see anything in a place she was unfamiliar with normally would have scared her out of her wits, she faced death in her dilemma, and so she was no longer afraid.

Fearlessly trekking down the stairs, she finally reached her destination, as she saw the grand piano, a glum lustre about it, shining through the dust under the light of her small flashlight.

Closing the last of the distance between her and one of the final memories of her life in Tokyo, she pulled out the piano bench and sat down, beginning to flex her fingers as if she were about to play a composition, perhaps one of the ones her mother had written and would never be able to replicate. But, no, she wasn't there to create music; rather, she was there to create a final bit of satisfaction for herself.

Opening up the lid of the piano, a long strip of red cloth was laid over the keys. The fabric floated gently over each and every one of the white keys with support from the black ones.

184

Careful with her touch, Autumn lifted the long blanket off of the keys, and they were exposed to her sight. Even under the dim light of the weak flashlight, she could see the brilliant faux ivory keys twinkling happily, as if each of them were diamonds shining under the light of the sun. The keys called out to her to play them – but she didn't have time to play them, she had to get back to school...

But I guess one song wouldn't hurt, Autumn thought to herself, her fingers already rested over the keys, prepared to play, the palms of her hands already slightly sweaty anticipating the song she was about to play.

Laying down her fingers on the keys, she tapped her feet lightly on the ground, again with that eerie echoing sound, and she began to play her piece, the 6th movement of the Kizuno Sonata. She knew that it was the final piece out of the six movements in the song that her mother and Mr. Chan had written. It was one of the last things that they had brought over from Japan, one of the last marks they had left in their hometown and in the hearts of their friends before they left for Perten.

The beginning of the piece sounded like the ending: she played the entire piece by memory, each stroking of a key just another note burnt into her memory by the vigorous practice sessions she had to undergo within the supervision of her mother.

Suddenly, she was interrupted by the bell of Perten Senior High, which rang exactly 10 minutes before the bell at Forest Peninsula High did. Reality hit her like a 10 pound brick.

Knowing she had to get to her own school, and the fact that she would soon be found by a student of this school who had to use the concert hall in first period, she recovered the red fabric and covered up the keys.

As she closed the lid over the keys of the piano, she knew that she was really only hiding all evidence that she existed, the fact that she had shown up and done anything in the concert hall.

Picking up her flashlight, she left the piano in the state she had found it, and fled the cradle of her memories in the loving embrace of the darkness for the cruel light of the outside world.

Chapter 29

The day finished in just about the same way it had started. The bells rang uniformly throughout the school, teachers held back some students, and they dismissed others.

Cindy and Damian got up from their desks in English, and joined the other students, all in a rush to leave the building to get to their weekends. The period had been rather monotonous like most others, and the entire hour and 20 minutes were devoted to exam review, as they were coming up next week.

Cindy sighed a little sigh, expressing her exasperation at the exams coming up so soon, and the fact that she was going to do rather badly on them. The gesture said it all: that she was worried about what would happen once her parents saw how she did - but Damian knew not to insist to help her. She would only insist against it until he had to give up.

Either way, what was the point in English if she could get a passing grade? It wasn't what she wanted to do in the future anyway. The distant future wasn't even in her sight yet, at least not at that moment, as she fished around in her bag's pocket, pretentiously casting her hand around, searching for the two small boxes.

As Damian watched Cindy reach into her pockets, deep in thought as she fumbled through the contents of the flap of her bag, he wondered what she was looking for. Every time he saw her that day, she seemed to sub-consciously think of whatever was in there, and reach in to check if it was still there, but the look in her eyes told him that she was going to do more than just check on the item this time.

Cindy's hand came out of the bag, no longer empty, but with two rings dangling by her finger – silver, maybe white gold to Damian's eyes – holding them outwards for Damian to see.

"Promise rings. For us. Um. Happy 4th year anniversary!" Cindy exclaimed to Damian, seeming almost breathless and at a loss for words after she presented the rings to him. Seeing that he also had no response to what she had just done, and was shocked beyond his comprehension She grasped his hand, separating his fingers with one of her hands, the other one placing one of the rings on his ring finger. It was on his right hand, which seemed to emphasize to him the idea of a "promise" ring, and so he seemed to calm down.

Damian slowly raised his arms a slight distance from his stomach and finally snapped back to reality, noticing the pressure of the cold metal ring pressing against his finger. It was beautiful, and the exact replica of it was less than a metre away from him, on Cindy's finger. The crafted metallic vines on the front of the ring seemed to be entwined tightly together, refusing to let go. The sparkle of the metal of the ring terrified him slightly though, made his heart skip a beat or two – what would other people think of him when they saw the ring?

The answer came to him very suddenly though as he realized: what did it matter what other people thought of the ring on his finger? It was a gift from Cindy, and he didn't mind showing everyone.

"Okay, we'll just drop by my house, grab my guitar, and we'll go meet Mr. Grey at the concert hall?"

"That's exactly what we're going to do," Cindy replied to Damian, squeezing him lightly around the waste and gripping his hand gently as they walked out of the school, awaiting their performance that night.

The loud sound of bells echoed in her mind, only a faint annoyance to her, interrupting her monotonous indulgence of the silence she had in her final period, English. Really, exams weren't a worry to her, so she tuned out, and thought of her plans for the night.

Autumn was dressed in semi-formal attire, not wanting to look so flashy that anyone would notice her, but not wanting to look so underdressed that she would have the same effect. Her clothes would let her blend in when she got to the concert hall, only 10 minutes away from her school if she walked.

Those 10 minutes were over in what seemed more like a second though, and that's how much time it felt like she had to think things over. Autumn stopped a short distance from the large black building where she had been that morning, and she could already see the piano inside, waiting to be played by another musician.

Autumn had only seen Cindy play once, and she remembered being shocked by how well the girl played the instrument: maybe it was time to let go, maybe *she* was the better one for Damian, not herself.

She sighed, wondering what would happen if she were to approach the concert hall early, to actually meet Cindy, get to know her and see what she was like. The opportunity was clear, and it would have been so easy for her to take it.

She remained sitting on a stone bench though, at least two blocks away from Perten Senior High, far enough away that no one would think she was there to see the performance. It was still only 3:00pm, a full hour at least before the first performance of the afternoon. Two hours before she would have to sit through the night, sweating away in her uncomfortable clothes, watching them perform. *Them.*

Chapter 30

Standing on the wide open stage, feeling as if there were at least a hundred pairs of eyes already rested upon him; Damian sat down and held his guitar close to him, resting it on his lap.

"Alright you two, let's do a quick run-through of this piece and see how it sounds, though I trust that you, Ms. Lau, have already insured that it be played well. After you finish running this through, we absolutely must go through my piece: you need to check out the new part I wrote for you, see if you like it," Mr. Grey stated out loud, not actually looking at anyone in specific, but rather was strenuously sorting through the piles of music he kept in his bag.

The perspiration running down Cindy's teacher's forehead truly put into perspective to all of the students how nervous he was, as water probably would have frozen over in the air conditioned stage. That made it so that in the summer, they always had a full audience, even if not everyone was there for the music.

Not waiting for his count, wanting to be efficient with the little time they had before their performance, a mere hour, Cindy and Damian began playing the piece immediately, and the chatter between the orchestral strings stopped. The room fell silent and the piece began, the musical notes drifting through the air and vibrating sullenly on anything that wasn't secured properly.

The two majestic musical instruments took the floor, and seized the small audience they had on the stage right at that moment, captivating each of them; the two musicians barely noticed.

The notes carried the senses of the people around them, alleviating the stress that they had, calming any nerves for the performance to come, and taking everyone higher and higher, through the dark ceiling of the old concert hall.

Each instrument's voice overlapped the other's quick succession of notes drawing the piece to an end, before anyone had fully comprehended the beauty of the beginning.

The short bout of applause that had come from the other instrumentalists, sitting in a row alongside the stage, was silenced by Mr. Grey. There was no time to applaud and cheer to congratulate the couple: they had to practice.

"Alright everyone, we're going to take this one from the top. You know what to do Cindy: take it away."

The pocket watch in her hand, just taken out of her bag, told Autumn that the time was exactly 5:05pm, right on the mark. She decided she would show up at the concert hall right then, and be a few minutes early for the first performance, so that she might get a decent seat.

The night had brought cool air upon the world, which she was grateful for, even in her last few moments. Approaching the door of the concert hall quickly, she shook the man's hand, *was Mr. Grey his name?,* saying a quick "hello", not making eye contact, before quickly swooping into the concert hall and out of sight.

It seemed like the instrumentalists were all just sitting there in fear and sinking in their own nerves, none of them feeling quite ready to perform. They had to be though, and she was pretty sure the teacher would have expressed that to all of them already: they had a show to put on, and it wasn't within their power to put it off.

This show would be the final act for her, and after she was done with it, she knew what she was to do, how she was to close the curtains on the story of her life...

Autumn sat in her seat, uncomfortably near another family, so she shifted over one, then two seats. She wanted to be alone and secluded from the rest of the people in the concert hall. No matter how much she *did* want to see her demise, her oh-so-dramatic demise, she didn't want people to see it as a work in progress. She only wanted them to know of her completed masterpiece.

She spent a good 20 minutes debating what had gone on in her life so far, feeling like the character from any generic movie thinking over the events of their life, a makeshift montage scene playing in her head – but it was interrupted by the announcement from Mr. Grey.

"Ladies and gentlemen, may I please have your attention?" he cleared his throat loudly away from the microphone after speaking one line, "We have decided to change the order of the pieces in our schedule tonight, and the first song that will be played for you was written by a young composer, one of our own at Perten Senior High, Cindy Lau!"

The crowd applauded politely, with traces of wolf whistles and cheers from some of her friends scattered throughout the masses of people also present. She smiled widely at them all, and took her cue to take the microphone and begin talking about her piece, as Autumn watched, feeling like the only member of the audience.

Cindy approached the front of the stage looking like she wanted nothing more than to just sit at the piano and start playing, but she still spoke to the crowd, her lines perfectly rehearsed in 10 minutes of preparation before they performed.

"The first piece that will be played tonight is, as Mr. Grey said, a piece written by myself." More cheers. "It's called Relentless Reminiscence, and is a duet between Damian Huong over there on guitar, and myself, on piano. I hope you all enjoy it, and the songs we will be performing later tonight." Further applause.

Too bad Autumn wouldn't hear anything more than that song.

Damian opened the piece, playing his first notes, just as they had rehearsed, the rising and falling of the notes was almost hypnotic, distracting Autumn as she took a minute to absorb the sheer beauty of the piece written by Cindy. She wasn't half-bad at writing music, Autumn was forced to admit.

If Cindy had helped her mother with the Kizuno Sonata... Autumn really wouldn't have minded playing it so much. The tension between her and Cindy felt resolved for a second – if Damian wasn't part of the equation, Autumn was pretty sure the two of them would have gotten along perfectly.

Too bad that wasn't the way it was.

The second voice of the song was added in such a subtle manner that Autumn barely noticed the whisper of the stroking in the piano. The strings and keys - all the mechanisms of the beautiful instrument sounded beautifully played, even by someone other than herself, and she credited Cindy yet again. The instrument that they both played... that kind of relation would normally spark competition between Autumn and the other person, constant challenges to see who could play better.

Too bad they wouldn't have the time to do that.

The song carried on, and Autumn felt the end impending upon her, the weight of the whole song drifting directly over her head, waiting to drop down upon her. She still tried to focus though, to absorb the full beauty of the song, played perfectly in beat to the fast, rhythmic beating of her heart.

Autumn closed her eyes, allowing the melody to flow through her, allowing her to lose control over herself, to relax for a moment, to put herself in Cindy's place. She had already seen the rings on both of their fingers, identical in shape, and evident that they had only been put on earlier that day. Damian uncomfortably pushed the ring up and down his finger, revealing there was no mark, no imprint of the metal band around his finger.

Too bad the other ring wasn't on her *finger.*

The piece continued, displaying clear structure to her, the guitar falling silent for the piano to take over, the piano quieting down for Damian's guitar to take dominance. When one instrument fell silent to allow the other a turn to speak, each of the musicians had something they did to pass by the time before they would have to play again.

Cindy would look at her ring, happily running her finger over it, watching her Damian – it hurt to think of it that way – play his part, to bring the melody back to a place where she could take over.

The whole song was a mutual agreement: each of the instruments would go half of the way, and meet the other one, only for a few seconds of brief conversation, before one was forced to be silent again. Those few seconds the instruments spoke in unison were enough to express how close they were though, and how close an ending was for the piece.

The notes of the song only foreshadowed the events to follow, and she was haunted by each and every tone coming from the two instruments. In any other scenario, Autumn would have been perfectly happy to show up to a performance and just enjoy the music presented by two skilled musicians, but this time, that wasn't the case.

Too bad there wasn't a piece to follow this one, a sequel to her life.

194

The chord changes happened faster, her heart beating quickly, following the motions of the piece perfectly, matching the rhythmic increases, until the final chords were struck, the ending mere seconds away. Autumn found her hand closing around the cold knife handle, wrenching it out of the depths of her bag, not being able to stand the feeling of anticipation of the ending anymore.

Too bad it hadn't been her.

Autumn raised the knife by its chilly metal handle, feeling the bitter cold against her skin, the guilt working its way in to her veins already: *what was she doing?* She didn't know, but she knew exactly what, also.

Not waiting to comprehend her thoughts, Autumn held the knife by the blade, like her grandmother did before her when it had gotten to be too much, the losses unbearable. Autumn plunged the freezing blade through her heart, gasping and letting go of the last breath she would ever take, releasing the last bit of pain she would ever feel and crying the last tear she would ever cry.

As the tear ran down her face, the final chord, a definite CMaj9 rang through her ears; each note was one more last word the world had for her. She still held the knife with her unfeeling hands, and the crowd applauded.

Too bad she wasn't the one for him.

"Bye, Damian…"

7312595R0

Made in the USA
Charleston, SC
16 February 2011